THE BLIND WORLD LITERALLY

THE BLIND WORLD... LITERALLY

V. S. SHIVAN

Unicorn Books Pvt. Ltd.
F-2/16, Ansari Road, Daryaganj, New Delhi-110002
• E-mail: info@unicornbooks.in

Edition: 2019

ISBN 978-81-7806-405-5 (Paper Back)

Cover Design: ....

www.unicornbooks.in

Printed: Param Offsetters, Okhla, New Delhi-110020

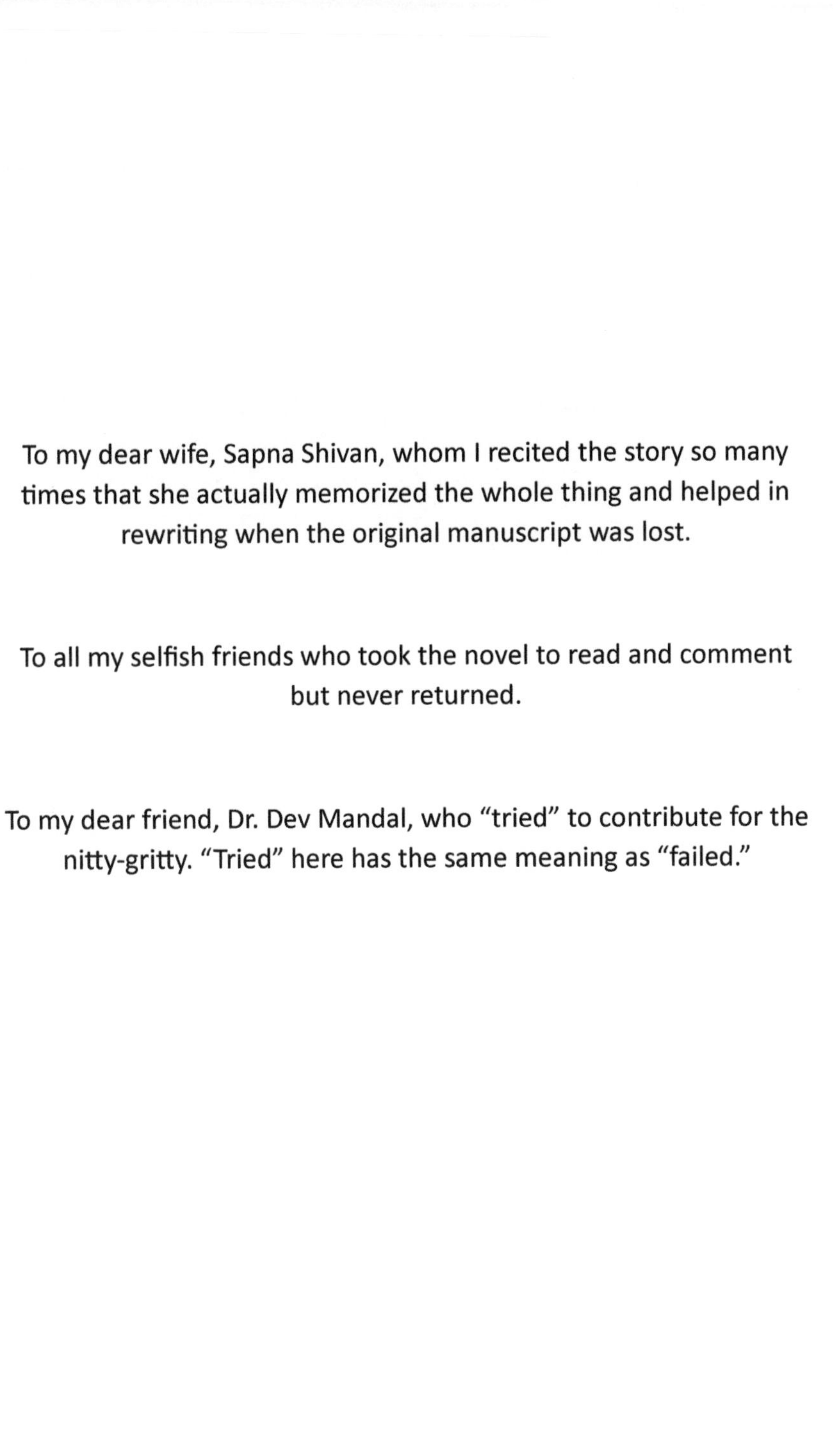

To my dear wife, Sapna Shivan, whom I recited the story so many times that she actually memorized the whole thing and helped in rewriting when the original manuscript was lost.

To all my selfish friends who took the novel to read and comment but never returned.

To my dear friend, Dr. Dev Mandal, who "tried" to contribute for the nitty-gritty. "Tried" here has the same meaning as "failed."

CONTENTS

Acknowledgement

When I was 12 years old, my elder brother, V.S. Satish, used to recite me bedtime stories. There was no TV, phone, or even much of story books in our house. I used to stare at his face watching all his expressions and intonations as he used to dramatize the whole situation. Those were the good old days when a real person narrated incidences and stories in front of you. I actually felt they were all real as he never disclosed the disclaimer. Apart from the once-in-a-while horror stories, I loved listening to him and would keenly wait for the nighttime to sit together. I still accurately remember a few of those and desperately miss those days when life was full of fantasies.

From his innumerable collection of too-weird-to-be-true stories, this story of the "Literal Blind World" thrilled me a lot. I often had dreams about it and this really triggered my imagination. By the time I finished high school, I had already recited the same story to many of my friends who found it equally fascinating. This got stuck in my head and I decided to write the whole story in "Hindi." I successfully completed writing the elaborative version during summer vacation. The manuscript rotated amongst my friends and eventually went missing. Life moved on and this priceless story got lost without any trace.

Presently, my 6-year-old daughter, Meenaxi Shivan, and my 2-year-old son, Sundaran Shivan, remind me of myself when they constantly demand a bedtime story every night. Sometimes my list of stories gets exhausted, but they are supportive enough to let me recite the same story again and again. Their mother is also helpful in taking over the narration when I am too tired. I am an avid reader and love to read any fiction book I can get my hands on. Still, this story remains the undisputed champion in my mind. Ultimately, after 15 years, I felt the desire to again write my own novel, this time in English, and let the world know of a story that is no less than a fairytale.

V.S. Shivan

LIGHTS!
CAMERA!
ACTION!

THE HUNGRY ARMY

Vanity vans of different news channels and press reporters had already clogged the *Jai Singh Road* situated in *Connaught Place,* popularly known as the heart of *New Delhi* (national capital of India). The queue extended till *Gurudwara Bangla Sahib*, the sacred religious place of *Sikhism*. Some policemen could be seen here and there directing journalists to their destination by hand-signaling, and also providing unrelated traffic the right of way. Everyone was headed toward the newly built *YMCA International Conference Center*.

Some media persons were already inside the building and many had lined up outside with the security guards having a tough time checking everyone's ID and letting them inside one-by-one. Some were even trying to barge in their vehicles by claiming they were from the so-called premier news channels and one mature security personnel helplessly kept telling them, 'not allowed as per order.' There was a small banner hanging on the *Ashoka* tree adjacent to the entry gate that read, "Press Conference for new novel – Byju."

Inside the jampacked conference hall, there were roughly 60 to 80 seats, all occupied by journalists with stereotype looks of photo IDs hanging around their necks, and majority of them fiddling pens or smartphones with writing pads on their laps. The place was so cramped that there were a lot of media persons standing behind the seating arrangements and also on the left and right walkways. The middle path was occupied by cameramen who had already set their cameras into position and were standing just next to their tripods waiting to start rolling.

Countless mics had mounted the desk in front of the speaker sitting in a chair on the dais who was waving his hands up and down as if asking everyone to settle down. The intertwined voices of journalists were very loud and unable to be deciphered except a few common words like 'sir,' 'please tell,' etc. The speaker stood up with his hands folded and said, *'namaste'*. He smiled as silence superseded the murmur and started his speech.

'Thank you all for taking your precious time out of the hectic schedule and coming here. I know how difficult it is for a news industry personnel to spare some moments on a writer's first novel and that too which is under construction. I believe my PR agency has done a great job being able to get you all present here today. I believe in appreciation more than appraisal, so I will write a 5-star feedback for them. Apart from the cocktail and non-veg buffet that will be provided in the *YMCA Dining Hall* at the lobby right after this press conference, if you have any specific questions related to my novel, I will be happy to answer and explain. By the way, my name is Byju! In case you missed it.'

Byju anxiously waited for anyone to respond. He could sense that the journalists were playing "you first" with each other.

One middle-aged expressionless reporter finally spoke, 'please explain about the book.'

Byju smiled with closed lips, adjusted his mic, and said, 'well, the book is all about the problems going on in the world these days and everyone turning a blind eye towards them. Everyone wants a Bhagat Singh or Mahatma Gandhi in the world, but no one wants their own children to be the one. Everyone admires the army men and their sacrifice for the country, but they want their children to do only office work which is considered to be safe. If someone sees an accident on the road, they will just curse others that no one is helping or calling the police, but they don't want to do it themselves in the first place to avoid any trouble. Houses are splitting because people want nuclear family. Their purpose of life is only to earn more and more, albeit without their own family members. Our legal system is so weak that even when a girl identifies the rapist in front of the judge before she dies of the cruelty she took and also the accused pleads guilty, it takes countless years just for the sentencing, let alone the punishment. If we catch a thief stealing, everyone will beat him to death even if the amount he stole was meagre, but if a big businessman or politician took away a major chunk of our country's development money, we don't even file a petition. Malnourishment is prevalent in our country, but tons of food is wasted in parties. I've seen ignorant people blocking the way of ambulance and fire brigades. Cheating and forgery are all-time high in today's society, so much so that even we have stopped trusting our own relatives. Heinous crimes are everywhere, and no one cares till it's their turn. And finally, when some pure soul comes out to help others or protest, we never support him. It ends either with his murder by the mafia or him being neglected by the society. So, that's my big question. Are we all blind? Can't we see what's happening? Can't we no longer judge what's wrong and what's right? The world has intentionally turned blind with ignorance and selfishness.' Byju took a deep breath as if to calm himself down.

Everyone got speechless. The truth opened their eyes to reveal the difference between being practical and reality. The pause denoted element of surprise and strong agreement.

A super-slim reporter commented, 'you are right sir. These days, when someone is fighting on the street, our first preference is to ignore and stay out of it even if the person involved is known to us. We even instruct our children and family members to close the doors and windows and not to go there.'

Byju agreed, 'yes, and that's considered to be the default and most acceptable behavior in today's society. No matter who is wrong and who is right, if it's a fight or protest, I'm not participating.'

A female reporter with a big red *bindi* on her forehead asked, 'you mentioned about nuclear family. Isn't that a personal choice? How come it's affecting the society?'

Byju raised his eyebrows to the silly question asked and replied, 'that's the root cause of all the problems ma'am. Firstly, the tendency to be alone or separate is in itself a big issue. If a person is taught or experiences this in childhood, he will not relate to his own family members, let alone the society. This will give birth to selfishness and of course ignorance of other's well-being in the long run. Society is a team effort where everyone should contribute towards mutual welfare. In fact, religious extremism and terrorism flourishes where children learn to separate and to be separate.'

Byju then turned his face toward a spectacled reporter wearing *kurta-pajama* who had his right hand raised and was waiting for the turn. The reporter noticed the cue and spoke, 'sir, you didn't mention about the widespread corruption in our country. Isn't that an issue as well?'

Byju started by saying, *'yeh bik gayi hai gormint.'* Everyone laughed. Byju continued, 'I forgot to mention in my intro speech, but of course I've written a lot about it in the book. Let's take the example of politicians. You might get bored when I ask you to compare their monthly income with their total worth, as you might have already heard this and calculated yourself multiple times in the past. Rather, I will just ask a few questions that will have the answer in itself. In any locality you go, tell me who owns the biggest and most expensive houses and properties? Was the individual this rich before he won the election? Also, everyone knows there will be distribution of money and benefits during the election time. Where does the money come from and why does a person want to spend this huge amount for a position which will legally yield him a salary less than a private firm's B-grade employee?'

Byju had the attention and silence of everyone present in the hall. After all, it was the oblivious reiteration.

'So, what do you suggest?' the same middle-aged expressionless reporter asked.

Byju smiled broadly and replied, 'well, that's what is under construction. I've the idea in my mind but am yet to write it down. I'd rather mention it here first. Just working on perfection in two aspects of the society can solve all these – Education and Legal System. Education will yield knowledgeable citizens with the power of questioning. An unflawed legal system will empower reliability and faith, thereby increasing responsibility. If a society has strong education and legal system, it will definitely grow and prosper.'

A reporter sitting in the front row asked, 'one final question sir. What's the name of the book and when are you going to launch it?'

Byju strengthened his voice so everyone could hear him, 'the tentative name of the book is *The Blind World*. Actually, I named it this way because even though people are not literally blind, they are acting as blind. As the saying goes, "*it's easy to show something to someone who is actually blind than to someone who doesn't want to see*." I will be launching the book by the end of this month.'

Byju anxiously looked around for further questions, concerns, or suggestions. There were none. Moreover, majority of the reporters were checking on their wristwatch for the time.

Byju folded his hands and said, '*namaskar*.' His eyes blissed as he could sense the journalists were really interested in his book, as some of them wrote notes in their respective writing pads before standing up. As everyone left the hall toward the *YMCA Dining Hall* in the lobby, Byju sat on the dais with all smiles and happy face. He took a sigh of relief turning to his friend, Rohit, who was all this time standing near the entry-cum-exit door of the hall and helping with crowd management. Rohit came running to the dais and shook Byju's hand while congratulating him.

'That was a killer speech man,' Rohit said with eyes wide-open in amusement.

'When you write a book, you should know all the aspects about it thoroughly,' Byju said with his eyes on a poster hanging on the farthest wall. He murmured something as if reading it.

Rohit asked, 'what are you looking at?'

Byju replied, 'you see that poster on the wall there?'

Rohit struggled to find it.

'*Arrey baba*! There, behind the sitting arrangement. What a great quote by Mahatma Gandhi *ji*, *"an eye for an eye will make the whole world blind"*,' Byju spoke as he pointed his finger at the poster on the wall.

Rohit tried to focus and make sense on what was written. He spoke on a low-tone voice, 'well, I can see that there is a poster there, but I can't really read what's written because it's too far of a distance to be read by any normal-eyed person. Your eyes must be very sharp.'

Byju pulled his earlobes and spoke with a naughty smile, 'God's gift. I don't take the credit nor the pride for that.'

Byju and Rohit giggled. Rohit took out his phone and captured a selfie. He noticed the time in the cellphone.

'Let's go and take some lunch *bhai*. We started late today, and it is already way past lunchtime now. Moreover, it will take a while to get our car out of the parking lot because of the rush outside,' Rohit said as he attempted to speed up the departing process.

Byju got confused and said, 'hey, wait! Don't we have lunch booked here?'

Rohit rolled his eyes and replied, 'brother, you can't see the obvious trouble here that I can foresee. We booked the buffet for 50-60 dignitaries, but I stopped counting after 100 who were present in the hall. Apart from that, we have cocktail also on offer. The reporters' intentions don't seem to go to work after this but rather gorge on the chicken and drinks till they pass out. *YMCA* is going to buy a new building with the likely amount due on us.'

Byju was about to say something when Rohit interrupted him and continued, 'also, you are a pure vegetarian and everything on buffet today is non-veg including the dessert which has egg as an ingredient. I'm sacrificing my *mutton tikka* and the prestigious *Royal Stag* just for you, so hurry up before I come back to my senses.'

Rohit was the kind of person who was both bulky and active. He looked like a heavyweight MMA wrestler. Calorie was his want and need. So, when he said gotta go, Byju hafta go.

The Scar

Byju waited at the gate and started reading the "dos and don'ts" written on a big banner board just outside the building. He smiled as he noticed someone had changed the hyphen in "To-Let" to an "i" with a marker or something. A loud squealing sound was heard, and Rohit brought his *WagonR* car out of the parking lot.

They took *Ashoka Road* from *Gurudwara Bangla Sahib* and just after two roundabouts and roughly 5 minutes' drive reached their destination – *Andhra Bhavan*. The otherwise rarely used *Jaswant Singh Road* served as the unofficial free parking space for all the unusually high number of visitors' cars and tourist buses. Fitting in a grey *WagonR* in the space of an autorickshaw was no big deal.

The state *Andhra Pradesh* had recently been split into *Andhra Pradesh* and *Telangana*, but the property was yet to be divided. So, there were two signboards of both *Andhra Bhavan* and *Telangana Bhavan* adjacent to the main gate. It didn't matter to the visitors coming there to lunch or dine as the canteen could only be accessed through the gate on the other side that was open for all.

From the main gate, Byju and Rohit had to walk around 100 meters to reach the canteen. Rohit commented the effort was next to nothing as compared to the incentives in eating there. Moreover, there was crowd waiting outside for their turn. So, Rohit bought token and they waited outside till the *thambi* shouted out their token number and assigned them seats. Obviously, Rohit didn't order any of the non-veg delicacies on offer. They purchased the veg South Indian *thali* with unlimited servings of rice, *puri*, four different curries, *sambar*, *rasam*, curd, sweet, and *papad*. There were countless waiters to provide any item to the customer's table instantly. Byju enjoyed the overall experience and taste of South Indian food and was amazed to know the subsidized price was unbelievably just $120 per person.

As Byju and Rohit were enjoying the meal with Rohit asking for refills again and again, Byju chuckled. Rohit also giggled as he ate like a man who had just arrived from the *Great Famine*. While Byju had finished, Rohit repeated the process of mixing rice and sambar with hand, making a ball, and putting it in his mouth. He chewed it while simultaneously creating another ball, and as soon as he gulped the rice ball, he would put the next ball in his mouth. This seemed like a vicious circle and took eternity to finish, but Byju couldn't do anything other than staring at Rohit and watching this recreational activity in action.

As they both were standing in queue to wash their hands, Rohit took a close look at Byju's face and said, 'I never asked this but why do you have a dimple on only one cheek? I haven't seen anyone else with dimple on single cheek before and that too at this peculiar location.'

Byju was constantly smiling perhaps because he just witnessed the extent to which one person can eat when he gets tasty food and that too unlimited for a mere cost. He noticed Rohit's inspection and replied, 'that's because it's not a dimple but more of a scar. When I was 9 years old, I slipped and fell with my cheek hitting on the sharp edge of a cemented stair. It pierced through but healed in a few days leaving a scar that looks like dimple. It has never bothered me and now as I have grown up, it actually looks nice on me as told by some of my well-wishers.'

'I think I can help you with this. My sister also had a scar on her eyebrow, which completely vanished with *Mederma* cream,' Rohit suggested.

Byju replied ignorantly, 'I don't want to treat this anyways. I'm happy with how I look. Thank you for the advice though.'

Rohit seemed consistent.

Byju tried to divert Rohit's attention, 'okay, buy me a *paan* from the counter. Andhra Bhavan recommends trying this for easy digestion of the truckload we just ate.'

'Sure *bhai*, but I will definitely gift you *Mederma* cream. It's worth it,' Rohit took an oath.

Byju helplessly nodded his head.

They bought the *paan* from the cash counter of *Andhra Bhavan* canteen. It cost only $10 for the mouth-watering betel leaf with something sweet inside.

As Byju and Rohit walked toward the car while chewing the *paan*, Byju explained to Rohit, 'in Indian tradition, betel leaf is consumed after food to help in digestion. There is a false belief that it should always be spat out after chewing and ingesting the juice, whereas it should always be swallowed unless you consume it with areca nut.'

As they boarded the car, Rohit spat on the road something that was red in color and liquidized in consistency, which was of course the aftermath of chewing the *paan* for a long time. As he closed the door and started the car engine, Byju's only wording was 'unbelievable,' before he took out his checkered handkerchief and placed on his face in order to sleep.

Rohit shook Byju with his hands.

'Let me sleep man. I'm tired and my stomach is fully packed. Let's go home and snooze,' Byju spoke as his hanky fell from his face and his eyes were closed.

'You forgot *bhai*. Today is our greatest friend, Alok's birthday. Like always, he has organized a private party amongst only us four friends and already bombarded my *WhatsApp*,' Rohit said while shaking Byju violently.

'Yeah I know. I switched off my phone at the start of the conference. After I wake up in the evening, I will call him,' Byju replied with his eyes still closed.

'*Whatev*. To be on the safe side, I'll pick you up from your home. Alok promised that this is going to be the greatest weekend ever of our life. He has a surprise planned for all of us and I want you to be present when we open the box of unexpectable,' Rohit announced as he drove off the car with Byju.

The Surprise Trip

In the evening, Byju and Rohit arrived at Alok's place. The *WagonR* car looked mediocre compared to the expensive sedans parked in that VIP street. *Tilak Nagar* was known for its glisten and glamour and this street was a true representative of the richest among the rich. All the houses had nameplates of builders, politicians, jewelers, one spiritual leader, online portal owners, etc. All the houses were on the left and there was a beautiful park on the right. The park was empty as only those living there were allowed in it and these *nawabs* never step on the street, let alone the park. There were only 12 houses in that lane with the road being closed from one end by the massive walls of a private school. Alok's house was second last in the queue with the last one being of *Hariphool – The Astrologer*, which of course had a lot of banners and posters everywhere.

Alok's father was a businessman owning a grand electric generator factory. His house was truly huge with a big wooden main gate. The carpet area measured 10,800 square feet and the designer house standing on it would have definitely cost more than *Taj Mahal*.

The Nepali gatekeeper saluted them and directed the car toward the designated parking space for guests. Byju noticed Pradeep's white pearl crystal shine *Fortuner* car already parked there. Pradeep was their fourth friend. Byju and Rohit walked into the main door. The door was open as was the case every time Alok was expecting them. They went inside of the should-have-been 7-star hotel and walked straight to Alok's room, which itself could defeat *Yash Raj* movie sets. Pradeep and Alok smiled broadly and Byju approached Alok to hug him and wished happy birthday. They all settled on the queen-sized round bed and chatted about how the press conference went.

'Don't worry about the buffet bill *jaaneman*. You just need to dishonor the cheque. My *papa* will keep the case pending for years till they settle for 10% of the total,' Pradeep said in a relaxed manner as if this was a piece of cake for his father who was an infamous lawyer and appeared frequently in news channels for his bold attitude.

'I don't want it that way. This will badly affect my *karma*. Moreover, I definitely am not willing to spoil my book's reputation if this comes out in the media,' Byju said protectively.

Alok added to support Pradeep, '*yaar*, what *karma* and reputation. We will buy big advertising slots in the media and warn them not to publish anything against the book. Simple!'

'Dear Alok, please allow me to handle this myself. I've the money and I'll pay all the justified bills. My complete concentration at this time is to get the book published and reach to a respectful number of individuals. Let's not deviate from this goal,' Byju said.

'*Bhai*, I think the suggestion of Pradeep and Alok are considerable,' Rohit tried to change Byju's perception.

'Okay, okay! Give me one week to try my wits. If after that I feel the need of anybody's help, I will be sure to tell. Till then, nobody tries to act Santa. Agreed?' Byju asked while staring at all the three faces.

'Agreed,' everyone said at once.

A servant knocked the door and said 'Alok *baba*, dinner is ready.' He looked like an international airplane pilot without the hat. Alok nodded and he disappeared.

Alok stood up and announced, 'let's eat first and then I'll disclose the big surprise. Mother and father are on a business trip to Dubai and I want this weekend to be truly unforgettable.'

Alok was the first to go towards the dining room, followed by the rest.

The bigger-than-life dining table had every item one could think of eating. Primarily, there were 4 veg *curries*, starters, and main courses of both chicken and mutton, fried fish, two types of rice, *tawa roti* popularly known as the Indian bread, salad consisting of 10 vegetables, and even 5 different types of desserts waiting on the side table to be served. This was the usual in Alok's home every time the four of them met, and Byju always asked him what happens to the leftover, to which Alok's pet-reply was his servants considered themselves extremely lucky every time there was a get-together. Rohit and Pradeep were eternal competitors in eating here. Byju's pure-veg preference was well-respected and taken care of by the world-class servants who sorted and tagged food for convenience. Alok himself only took a couple of pieces from non-veg starters and his main course was soup followed by fruit pastry.

After dinner, they all sat on the U-shaped sofa in the living room to enjoy *Dom Pérignon* champagne, specially bought for Alok's birthday. Byju would always complement Alok that the room was so luxurious that perhaps middle-class living rooms should be called just-surviving rooms. Also, the golden U-shaped sofa looked like it must have been once a property of *Queen of England*. It was always a question for Byju as to why the hell do the rich have so big and sparkling chandeliers as if they were found in the secret chambers of *Padmanabhaswamy Temple*. The only thing a middle-class man was concerned while buying a chandelier, apart from the cost, was how difficult it will be to clean.

Alok tapped a glass of champagne with a spoon to seek everyone's attention.

'Time for my birthday speech. As you all know that for me, you're the only three friends I have from my childhood. In the last three years since we all passed out from *Venky College*, we only meet occasionally and that makes me feel damn lonely. I know that we all have different family obligations and our lives might not necessarily be together, but I want to cash in the opportunity of my parents not being here and the mandatory wish-granting guarantee that I have from all of you all as it's my birthday. You didn't bring any gift for me as you take me for granted, so I took you reciprocally granted and planned a trip to the *Himalayas*. I hope you will fulfil my wish and accompany me to the heaven on earth.' Alok completed the speech and waited eagerly for response.

Of course, nobody could deny him as no one actually brought a gift. Moreover, they didn't want to hurt Alok by ignoring his petty wishes.

Rohit the brave soul asked Alok, 'we still have so many wonderful foreign locations to visit, why do you want to go to *Himalayas* and where exactly?'

'It's a secret and I'll only disclose when we reach *Nainital*. You can consider this secrecy as my add-on wish,' Alok replied to Rohit while announcing to everyone.

'As you wish dear. Today is just Monday. Let's meet this Friday evening and depart,' Byju said.

Alok made a naughty face and said, 'well Byju, there is a teeny-tiny thing I forgot to mention in my wish specifications. By weekend, I meant not traveling on weekend but traveling till weekend. It's kind of a trekking and will take 3 to 4 days alone to reach the destination, so we start today and get back here by most probably Sunday night.'

Pradeep started laughing cynically. While Rohit was neutral, Byju had a big how-is-it-possible on his face. All three expressed their concerns and tight schedule for the weekdays and requested Alok to keep only realistic expectations like traveling to a normal location within the weekend itself. Alok obviously presumed this behavior.

'Oops! I think I missed one clause of the wish-granting treaty. I know that if I insist, you will be happily accompanying me and adjusting your schedule accordingly, but I also know the fact that it is almost impossible for me sometimes to get all of us together at one place due to our different work. Today's opportunity of unity I dearly don't *wanna* miss, so I've readied the driver and booked everything in advance. Guys, we need to start our journey right now and did I tell you that no phone or laptop allowed during this trip?' Alok leaned back as if resting his case.

'No way.' 'Are you out of your mind?' 'What are you saying?' Alok heard voices coming from everywhere.

Alok stood up and came to the front.

'We can information our parents tomorrow morning. It's no big deal as they know you are with me and we as friends usually go on trips together and many times spend the night at my home. Neither of us does any regular job, so leave from office can be ruled out. I don't see any obvious reason why you are saying no to these potentially wonderful moments we will be spending together, maybe the last time. Who knows where our lives will take us and whether we will meet like this again or not. Therefore, with a heavy heart, I've to say this – it's now or never. Whosoever leaves the house tonight shall never hear from me again.' Alok was both sad and angry. He went back to his room and laid on the bed staring at the ceiling.

The three unwilling souls just sat on the sofa in the living room and gave it a deep thought. After some time, they started talking softly. There was no question that Alok was right in whatever he said, and it was just for the rat race of bread and butter that they were saying no to a friend who truly loved them. After not much of a discussion and not much of a choice either, all three came to Alok and stood in front of him with hands on their waist and eyebrows lifted.

Alok's eyes stared the three pairs of eyes for a while. Alok was initially confused but suddenly his eyes became wide-open and a broad smile came on his face. He said in a fast-paced manner, 'oh! That you don't worry. We'll buy clothes and other necessities on the route. I've planned everything.'

Everyone laughed out loudly. Byju hugged Alok and whispered in his ears, 'only for you buddy.'

As Rohit and Pradeep rolled on the floor laughing and clapping, Alok took the intercom and ordered, '*Pajero nikaal*.'

The Death Wish

Alok's new car was *Pajero*. Though he was popularly known as the *Jaguar* guy in *Venky*, he technically bought this new car only for the long journey the four friends were about to undertake, and also because the sports version was launched just a few days ago with eye-catching advertisements all over the city.

They started at 12:30 in the night and reached *Nainital* by 7 a.m. Obviously, everyone slept throughout the journey except the driver whom Byju peeped whenever the car jumped on a speed breaker. Byju himself couldn't find much sleep amidst the rollercoaster ride. The driver, Chaudhary, was once a bouncer in an infamous pub in *Hauz Khas* and appointed by the parents of Alok as his bodyguard-cum-driver. When Alok was not traveling, Chaudhary could be seen sitting outside and smoking *hookah.* The calculative mind of Byju gave him a clear idea that if this 7-foot man ever turned wicked, the four friends didn't have a chance. Chaudhary, however, was tender-hearted and followed every command of Alok religiously.

As Alok had preplanned the whole trip, the car stopped right in front of *Season Resort Nainital*, a 5-star hotel. It took a while for everyone to get back from sleep and come out of the car. As soon as Byju opened the door, he felt the chilling cold and ran straight inside the hotel. The lobby was warmer because of the heaters installed. The rest three friends followed the same pattern.

A waiter then brought them to the premium room. It had a marvelous view of the *Nainital Lake* and the big glass walls made the experience mind-blowing. Alok told the waiter to bring the breakfast, to which the waiter obliged and was back within no time. It was for sure that Alok had pre-booked this as well as there was no menu selection process undertaken. Of course, all the items that a 5-star hotel could possibly serve for breakfast were present in the giant luxurious room. A major part of the last night's food was already in their stomach, but still they managed to take a bit of everything followed by hot *Ghorakhal* tea. As Rohit and Pradeep were busy stuffing up calories for the apocalypse, Byju approached Alok and softly asked him his plans.

'We're going to the *Roopkund Lake*,' Alok said with a welcoming smile.

Rohit and Pradeep suddenly stopped eating as if somebody had played the game *"statue."* They didn't look up as if they knew they were sitting ducks in the butcher shop. Byju couldn't believe what he just heard, and his expression was as if the judgement day had finally arrived. His Adam's apple shifted gears and he tried to reason with Alok.

'*Roopkund Lake*? The lake where more than 200 skeletons were found, and many are supposedly lying at the bottom. The mystery of the skeletons is still unresolved after 100 years of discovery. It is the ghastliest place in the world. Moreover, the lake itself is situated in the uninhabitable range of *Himalayas*, approximately 17,000 feet altitude. If we get stuck there, we will die of the freezing cold,' Byju said with the face of a person who has just received a capital punishment sentence.

Alok seemed unimpressed with Byju's argument. Rohit and Pradeep giggled. Like tears of happiness, these were giggles of fear.

'Yes, the great skeleton lake. This will be the adventure of our lifetime. I want to go there at any cost and also want my friends to experience the thrill,' Alok said while imagining a swim in the lake already.

'You willfully auto-corrected thrill my friends with kill my friends. My mother always told me not to befriend rich kids. I dearly miss my mother today,' Byju felt helpless.

All the three friends hugged as if acting to console each other and then high-fived Alok by shouting out loud together – 'let's face the gallows.'

THERE'S NO GOD

After everyone informed their parents about their whereabouts and plans, Pradeep insisted on visiting the revered *Naina Devi Temple* for blessings before they start their journey, to which everyone agreed. Byju recommended taking a nice bath at that time as *Roopkund* trek might be too cold.

All four wore *lohi* shawls brought by Chaudhary on behest of Alok. It was sufficiently warm and comforting. When asked why, Chaudhary explained it as the best cold protector in his home town, *Haryana*. Of course, it had become a uniform for Chaudhary in *Delhi* as well.

The main temple was located on an edge of the famous *Naini Lake*. According to *Hindu Mythology, Lord Shiva* was carrying his wife *Sati's* dead body toward *Kailash Mountain*. *Goddess Sati's* eyes fell on this place and the temple was established with two eyes inside the temple representing *Naina Devi*.

After worshipping, Rohit wanted to buy some trekking clothes from the nearby mall, to which everyone else thought the shawls would be sufficient enough. Alok spoke over the phone with someone and then asked Chaudhary to set the *MapMyIndia* GPS location to *Kathgodam Railway Station*.

Kathgodam was a town immediately north of *Haldwani* and only 1-hour from *Nainital Lake*. They reached there at noon, and after a few telephonic conversations of 'I'm here,' 'I'm standing in front of this gate,' and 'what are you wearing,' they were able to locate the person. Alok introduced him as Bahadur, the best trekking guide in all of *Uttarakhand*. Bahadur smiled modesty and asked everyone to get in the car and rush to *Lohajung* as it was expected to be midnight by the time they reached there. Bahadur sat in front to assist Chaudhary with the route.

It was the longest car ride for the four friends, around 12 hours including the 30-minute break for lunch in a *dhaba* near the *Kosi River* and 45 minutes for dinner near the blustery *Pindar River*. The snow-capped mountains kept coming closer and closer as they arrived *Lohajung*, a tiny little hamlet in *Chamoli* district. During the journey, many revelations came forth like the *Roopkund* trek being banned by the government due to safety hazards. This was duly conveyed by Bahadur to Alok many days ago, to which Alok's reply was he doesn't think any good-for-nothing government official was going to come all the way up to *Roopkund* just to fine or arrest them. Upon hearing this in the car, Rohit said, 'my grandma always told me that heaven was in the *Himalayas* and one day we will be going there definitely, either in this life or the afterlife.' This made everyone cheer.

Bahadur instructed Chaudhary toward a small cottage in *Lohajung* village. It was Bahadur's own house, which was partially a guest house as well. The cottage looked old but was well-furnished and had moderate mattresses. It was extreme cold at midnight, but the four friends were so tired and sleepy that they just jumped onto the bed and started snoring. Bahadur helped them with the comforters and closed the doors. The lengthy room with two double-beds was comparatively warm because of the wooden architecture. Bahadur offered Chaudhary a drink and asked him to sleep in his room.

Byju woke up with the soft noise Bahadur was making in order to awaken Alok. Alok looked like a person who was easily offended when awakened from sleep, so Bahadur restricted himself to no-touching and only a few low-tone 'sir *ji*' again and again. Maybe *Chanakya* wasn't familiar with Alok when he wrote the quote – "*the serpent, the king, the tiger, the stinging wasp, the small child, the dog owned by other people, and the fool: these seven ought not to be awakened from sleep."*

Bahadur told Byju that they need to start trekking now as it's a long way up the *Himalayas* and he doesn't want them to get stuck at nighttime between landmarks. Byju checked his phone and it was 6 a.m. He was too sleepy himself and felt chilling cold. He wrapped himself with the comforter and asked Bahadur to prepare tea for everyone. After a few attempts, Byju was able to awaken the *Kumbhakarnas*.

After tea, everyone felt a bit relieved with the still-insufficient warmth derived. Bahadur clarified that they needed to purchase trekking outfit from the local store, to which everyone shiveringly agreed and followed him with the comforters still on. They bought jackets, hand gloves, caps, and shoes and packed themselves airtight, windproof, and cold-resistant.

They went on to eat *aloo paratha* and mango pickle from the *Patwal Lodge*, which Bahadur had arranged well in advance. Of course, Bahadur had to intervene in the relishes of Rohit and Pradeep to keep them light for the tedious hike. Everyone walked to the temple at *Ajan Top* and sat on the wall-less room next to it to enjoy the scenic meadows and *Maiktoli Glacier*. Bahadur took out his to-do list and started discussing the process.

'*Sahib ji*, our destination is *Roopkund Lake* which is approximately 16,000 feet altitude. To get back here by Saturday, we will need to reach there by Friday, i.e., the third day from today. Only myself will be with you during the whole journey. I am born and brought up in this land, so you don't worry about a thing including food and shelter during our hiking. There is no use carrying your phone, watch, or any other electronic device beyond this point as it will stop working in the severe cold ahead. I suggest you keep all of your belongings in the car including your wallets as I have already made all the arrangements for the trek. I will carry the necessitations in my backpack and the only thing you will ever carry is the hiking pole, which will be provided when we start our climb. Also, as a precautionary measure, my home landline number and address will be written on your wrist. The ink seems permanent but vanishes automatically after 15 days. This is the unofficial nonnegotiable policy for off-records trekking. There is not much of flora or fauna to be seen at the lake but the beauty and mystery itself is mesmerizing. As we are a small group, there is no question of getting lost or separated. *Doctor Brandy* will be the only medicine available during the journey. May *Kalu Vinayak* bless us with a successful expedition.' Bahadur spoke fast as if he had recited the same thing many times in the past.

Bahadur proceeded to write his contact details on everyone's wrist. It felt like everyone was taking the oath to not back-off from the journey under any circumstances. Alok took Bahadur to a corner and whispered something in his ears, to which Bahadur replied in a neglectful fashion. Byju overhead Bahadur's response, 'I already told you sir not possible. These are not the places meant for this activity... Okay! I'll only tell when we reach there but don't blame me for any mishaps.'

'What's that Alok? Please no surprises henceforth,' Byju asked suspiciously.

'It's the last surprise. I promise! When the time comes, I'll disclose. I'm sure you all will love it,' Alok said with a broad smile and wink.

'There's no God,' Rohit said looking at the sky and then walked to the car. Everyone else followed and the excursion started.

World's Highest Green Carpet

They left *Lohajung* in car at 9 a.m. and reached *Wan* at approximately 10 a.m. It was a small village with a cluster of houses and cemented trail. The car stopped in front of a cluster of old cypress trees that were extremely thick. Bahadur asked the four friends to step out of the car as it was the farthest a vehicle can go, and the real trekking started from here. Bahadur took out 5 hiking poles and his massive backpack that was almost bigger than him. He seemed absolutely comfortable with this truckload on him as he ran on a short trail toward a small temple and rang the bell, which he told locals believed would ensure a safe trek. Alok instructed Chaudhary to go back to Bahadur's house in *Lohajung* and stay there until they arrive. They took a group selfie and then handed their phones, watches, wallets, etc. to Chaudhary for safekeeping.

Suddenly, Rohit took out a small brown paper bag while searching in his pocket. He thumped his head as if saying, 'how could I forget this?' Byju asked him what it was.

'This is the *Mederma* cream *bhai*. You remember I'd promised I'll gift this for your cheek's scar-cum-dimple. This is the bestseller product in my chemist shop. I put it in my pocket to give to you when we get in Alok's place, but so much happened that I completely forgot about this,' Rohit said as he handed the paper bag to Byju.

'If you say something, you'll do it regardless of the choice of others. Still, you're my friend and I'll accept this, though I'm not going to use it as I like my unique single-cheeked dimple. Please don't force me to use it now,' Byju said while taking the cream pouch.

'I love you *bhai* and that's why I do things that I think will benefit you,' Rohit said as he was getting touchy.

'I know you love me. Please do a favor, love me less,' Byju said feeling helpless.

Bahadur saw the emotional drama and intervened.

'You can keep it *Sahib ji*. At least, it will help your skin moisturize in the harsh cold weather uphill.' Bahadur said in a negotiating manner.

Byju was out of excuses. He unchained his long jacket and inserted the cream pouch in its innermost pocket. It seemed like he was sure this will go unused during the whole journey. Rohit was all smiles and satisfied with the gesture.

Bahadur waved goodbye to Chaudhary as the vehicle reversed and left. He gave the hiking pole to the four friends and had one for himself. He led the way on the trail straight ahead to the ridge. As was with the visual illusion during all mountain climbing experiences, the ascent looked short but took a long time to complete. It took 45 minutes to ascend from *Wan* to *Ranaka Dhar*, which meant "flowing blood," believed to be of demon *Lohasur* who was killed by *Goddess Parvati* in a battle there. Bahadur informed everyone that this was the shortest climb of the *Roopkund* trek and the others will be of few hours each.

Next, was a short descent to the gurgling *Neel Ganga*. The bridge on the river had an excellent view with trees overhanging the river and the water tripping and falling over boulders in the shade. Bahadur filled a 5-liter can from there, which he acknowledged will suffice for the day.

From there began the beautiful ascent through oak and rhododendron forests. The path was strewn with dry leaves that crunched and crackled beneath the trekking shoes. There were walnuts, pears,

Himalayan roses, and other flora. They even spotted a flycatcher and magpie on their 3-hour trekking to *Gharoli Patal*, which ended with a welcome sight of the magnificent *Mount Trishul*.

It was 2 p.m. and the four friends were more hungry than tired. There was a small hut with an old man inside. Bahadur went in and chatted with him in the local language. It took the old man and Bahadur 1 hour to cut the vegetables, light the firewood, and prepare rice and vegetable stew for all. This break plus the awkwardly delicious food gave the group enough energy to brave for the next landmark.

It was a steep climb of about half-an-hour on ascending stoned steps. The trail opened up to a huge meadow. They took the right trail into the forest of oak and rhododendrons. It took 2 hours to finish the forest trail and reach to the largest, greenest rolling carpet ever laid out on earth that was called *Auli Bugyal*. Acres and acres of green meadow scooped out of the mountainside, and all tiredness was forgotten in the mesmerizing sight of clouds drifting from below and gliding over the ridge.

It took another 1 hour to reach *Bedni Bugyal*, which was 5 km away and a mildly descending trail initially. The grass felt like carpet in the beginning of the trail. The majestic *Nanda Ghunti Mountain* was simply breathtaking. There was a short switchback climb of 20 minutes at the end of *Auli Bugyal* before the trail leveled out to a gentle trail to *Bedni Bugyal*.

It was already dark when they reached, and Bahadur guided them inside a campsite with makeshift tents, bonfire, mules standing by, and food being prepared in large utensils. There were no visitors except this group. They were offered tea followed by heavy dinner. At the bonfire, the cook told them *Auli* and *Bedni Bugyals* were Asia's largest high-altitude meadows. He advised going to a place that can be reached by a steep climb of around 1 hour, which provided a panoramic bird's eye view of the whole place as well as *Mount Neelkanth* and *Chaukhambha*. Obviously, this group wasn't interested in anything except reaching *Roopkund Lake* as soon as possible and Bahadur was kind enough to convey this to the cook.

This time, Bahadur informed only Byju that they will have to leave even earlier than before to finish the next day's journey in time. Byju nodded and asked Bahadur to only wake him up in the morning and he will get everyone ready on time. Everyone went inside their respective tents and slept soundly.

Kalu Vinayak

Byju woke up due to the sound produced by the bell tied around a mule's neck. He opened the tent's zip and the mule came toward him. The mule was more interested in grazing the soft green pasture grasses. Bahadur was already standing a few feet away watching the spectacular Himalayan peaks. As he was always, Bahadur seemed all packed and ready to take his clients to their destination. Byju came out and the view was the most picturesque moment to a photographer.

'*Sahib ji*, today's journey will be shorter and easier but colder. It will reach up to 0 degree Celsius at our last landmark for today. If everything goes well, tomorrow we will reach *Roopkund*. Please wake up Alok *sahib* and others and get ready in an hour,' Bahadur told Byju.

Byju conveyed the same and everyone came out of their respective tents still tired from yesterday. They all started brushing their teeth and Rohit was the first to use the makeshift toilet tent. The whole tent started trembling amidst the strong winds flowing around. The horrific sound of the gusty wind made poor Rohit to hold the tent with both hands from inside as if to prevent it from getting blown away. Pradeep commented, '*rehne do babua, tumse na ho payega*.' Everybody started laughing, even the cook, Bahadur, and the mule. After answering the nature's call and fury, Rohit came out as if he had just conquered a war.

The cook prepared *Maggi* and tea for breakfast inside the only shop situated at *Bedni Bugyal*. Pradeep was not satisfied and took some biscuits with him. They were all excited to know that now they will be riding on mules to their next stopover, *Pathar Nachuni*. Bahadur, however, walked ahead to guide them.

The trail to *Pathar Nachuni* climbed out of the *Bedni Bugyal* in a gradual meander. The trail could be followed through eyes for a few kilometers before it turned to the other side of the ridge. They climbed the slope behind the *Bedni Kund* and then reached to the main trail coming from *Auli Bugyal* to *Roopkund*. The trail now became clear and plain, but there were lots of muddy patches at the path due to the melting of snow on the way.

After reaching the other side, there was a gradual descent on the trail. Bahadur stopped at a site where the meadows merged to the alpine. This was *Pathar Nachuni*. He told everyone to walk from here as the mules were not allowed to go further due to the terrain and climatic conditions. Alok pursued him to no avail as Bahadur told him the mules are the primary source of livelihood to the locals and there was no way they were going to endanger them. Moreover, the place itself was known as *Ghora Lotani*, meaning "horse come back."

There were some snow patches here and there, which amused the four friends. Bahadur told them this was nothing as compared to what lied ahead. There was increased coldness in the air and a sense of isolation at the site. *Maggi* lunch was offered from a comparatively smaller shop than *Bedni Bugyal*. Alok was unimpressed, but Bahadur convinced him that better food will be available at the final landmark for the day. Instead, they settled for eating a heavy dinner tonight for better sleep.

Bahadur informed everyone that the path from here was very treacherous and dangerous with full of life-threatening snow patches till *Kalu Vinayak*. Even a single mistake could become lethal and drag them deep down in the gorge. The air would become thinner as they climb upward in this steep trail. Though the distance wasn't much, climbing this section should be very slow as any ways they were expected to reach the top in comfortable time. Getting breathless or even feeling dizzy was the commonest symptom among most trekkers here and it was highly recommended to take a 10-minute break every 15 minutes to acclimatize to the *Roopkund* altitude yet to come.

Except Alok, the rest three friends had an expression that equaled, "as if we have a choice."

The trail was zigzag and hence made them gain height very rapidly. Bahadur was helpful in instructing everyone to take adequate breaks and also to take care on some snow patches where the snow was sinking to knee-deep level. They skirted around these patches, but rest of the journey was moderate till mild snowfall occurred. All of them were witnessing a snowfall for the first time. Rohit was unable to speak due to the cold weather and was mumbling to himself. Byju got worried, to which Bahadur told Byju that Rohit's body was adjusting to the increased height and lack of oxygen. Rohit got scared but gradually his speech senses came back as he repeatedly mumbled the word "*goosfraba*" to calm himself down, which was suggested by Bahadur.

Climbing was a thrill and every time they looked up and took a bend on the trail, the ridgeline got closer and inspired them. Below, they could follow the trail that they took from the first saddle over *Ghora Lotani*.

Just before reaching the top, Bahadur excitedly shouted, *'Jai Shri Ganesh.'* He hand-gestured everyone to come running. Suddenly, all the scenery changed. All they could see was an endless white carpet of snow everywhere. The whole experience was overwhelming and awesome. This morning they were standing on the green carpet of meadows in *Bedni Bugyal* and now a white carpet of snow was welcoming them. The friends just stood there to digest the awe-inspiring moment.

Kalu Vinayak was a small temple dedicated to *Lord Ganesha*. The temple got its name from the black *Ganesha* idol enclosed in a stone shrine with lots of temple bells. Here, trekkers took blessing from *Lord Ganesha* for their safe and successful *Roopkund* trek.

Everyone paid obeisance by praying and donating the biscuits brought in by Pradeep from *Bedni Bugyal*. Beside the *Kalu Vinayak* shrine and right next to it started the first patch of snow toward the endless white carpet.

Trail from there was an easy-peasy piece of cake. It was gently down-sloping and fully covered with snow. It was easy to judge that the four friends were walking on snow for the first time and this celebration would be cherished for their whole life. Though the air was thin, and they were forcing their body to take deep breaths repeatedly, they felt delighted by sinking their shoes in the snow while walking. It was perhaps the best 2-kilometer walk they ever had.

It was twilight at *Kalu Vinayak* and dusk then at *Bhagwabasa*. Bahadur duly informed everyone that this was the resting place for the day and the next morning they will be at *Roopkund*, to which everyone sighed of relief. They had reached *Bhagwabasa* amidst the snowfall and bad weather.

Amazingly, *Bhagwabasa* had a cluster of stone huts booked for them. This area was completely isolated with no sign of flora or fauna. There was only one local there who also cooked dinner for them. It was too cold for the four friends to withstand and Bahadur gave them everything from his backpack to cover. He also provided polythene bags to wrap around their feet for insulation from snow-wet shoes.

It took around half-an-hour for them to relish the unknown delicacy. All four asked for refills as they had not eaten properly throughout the day and also because it was too delicious. Bahadur was unable to translate in English the ingredients dictated by the local. No one cared what it contained except Byju who confirmed it as a veg recipe.

The whole group sat encircling a bonfire inside an empty stone hut. They discussed how they first felt hearing about the trek and now they appreciate Alok's efforts and choice of the best place in the world. They all took an oath of being friends forever and going on a trip every six months. Alok suggested he plan the trip every time and keep it a surprise like this one. The other three were unconvinced and speechless.

Alok's eyes drenched when he mentioned he always dreamt of all of them working together, but there was no business that required a lawyer, a chemist, a generator factory owner, and a writer at one place. All four of them got emotional and hugged. Rohit started singing, *'yeh dosti hum nahin todenge, todenge dam magar tera saath na chhodenge...'*

One stone hut had two individual beds. It took some time and effort to drag in a third bed into the desired stone hut where all the four friends wanted to sleep together. The togetherness was caused more by the freezing cold than brotherhood. They installed their sleeping bags inside and used the beds as insulators from bottom.

Byju felt extreme cold and hardly slept the whole night making speculations of an unsolicited avalanche or snowstorm due to the windy snowfall and bad weather that ensued. There was both fear and excitement inside his heart when he realized how small a man was in the vast universe. Finally, he slept with the outside temperature running in negatives.

THE ROOPKUND LAKE

Byju slowly opened his eyes and noticed that the morning sunlight had illuminated the stone hut. The door was open and the rest three were outside playing snowball fight. The snowfall had stopped, and the sky cleared. There was a negligible wind though. Byju's body was stiff as if he had literally slept on the snow all night. He stretched a bit and asked Bahadur why the whole trek till now was kind of empty, to which Bahadur replied it was the cold season and locals moved to the meadows during this time of the year. Also, the *Roopkund* trek had been banned by the government and nobody came this far anyways.

Byju asked for some water and tried to help himself to grab the bottle from the side-holder of Bahadur's bag that was kept aside. The water and even the whole bottle had frozen and became solid as a rock. Bahadur saw this and told Byju informatively that the temperature in daytime is next to 0 degree Celsius. The only source of drinkable water was digging up the snow and melting it. The cook handed over a glass of hot water to Byju, which he gulped rapidly for the fear of freezing it too. Everyone was laughing, and Rohit showed thumbs up to Byju.

It was the summit day. The cook took some powdery substance from a container and poured it on hot water to prepare a delicious soup that was very thick and filled up everyone's stomach. Rohit and Pradeep of course needed refills, which Bahadur recommended not to no avail. No one could really figure out what it was actually made of, but they were happy to know it was vegetarian as per the translation from Bahadur.

Bahadur and the cook helped the four friends put on crampons – a traction device that was attached to the footwear to improve mobility on snow during ice climbing. Bahadur didn't wear one and only grabbed an ice-axe. The cook got busy stuffing forcefully aluminum rods, bundles of rope, and long pieces of heavy clothes into Bahadur's bag. He was constantly murmuring in his local language, *Garhwali*, to Bahadur as if complaining to him. Bahadur acted arrogantly toward him and shouted something, which was of course not understood by the friends at all but seemed like it meant, "mind your own business" or "let me do my job," as per the body language and hand gestures of Bahadur. Byju inquired about this, to which Alok jumped in and said it was the final surprise of the trip.

Byju, Rohit, and Pradeep got suspicious and couldn't take it anymore. They wanted to know if Alok was planning to spend the night at the bewitched lake. Alok first told them that the surprise will be more delightful. He proceeded to remind them of their promise to come and complete this trek in its fullest. Lastly, he reminded Byju about the question Byju asked during the whispered conversation between him and Bahadur at the *Ajan Temple* in *Lohajung* and how he had told Byju then that the surprise will be revealed in time. Alok told everyone that they were still 5 kilometers away from the surprise.

Rohit spoke, 'let's go and meet *Lord Shiva*. I can't even get my last wish fulfilled here, which is to meet *Sunny Leone*.'

Byju was totally surprised by the way Alok was planning his surprise. Byju waved his hand to Bahadur to lead the way and they started walking in a line carefully stepping only on the foot marks of Bahadur.

The snowfall last night had made the snowy slopes both slippery and dangerous. At multiple places, they just slid and rolled down on the slope, which was an enthralling experience for them, but Bahadur came running every time to help anyone who had slid and asked them to be careful. The four friends became serious with the safety only when Bahadur said, 'maybe the skeletons in the *Roopkund Lake* are the remnants of all the people who slid and ended up there, you never know.'

Initially, the climb was gradual and easy but slow due to the knee-deep snow. The snow changed into solid ice toward the end of the trail, which was a steep ascend. The crampons and a series of switchbacks helped them to gain height. The air was so thin at this altitude that they were all breathing rapidly with their mouths open. Their tiredness was fighting the battle of wits with the erect mountain. The last 10 minutes was intricate and even Bahadur had to use the four limbs to climb up to the snowy flank. There was no view until they all reached over the edge and the *Roopkund Lake* was right there. Kudos to all!

The view of the *Roopkund Lake* was truly mesmerizing. Everyone felt the divine magical vibration in the surrounding and ran the trail down 50 feet in a celebratory manner to actually reach to the lake. The whole area looked like a crater on the mountain face as it resembled the epicenter of an explosion site. Byju acknowledged that the lake was indeed bigger than what most internet pictures suggest. Surrounding the lake was all snow and mountain. Bahadur told it was 16,000 feet altitude here. Breathing was really a task for everyone.

Bahadur explained, 'the "Skeleton Lake," as the *Roopkund Lake* is popularly known, has intrigued many historians from the time around 300 human skeletons were discovered in the lake in 1942. The carbon dating placed the time of mass death around the 9th century AD. Along with the skeletons, wooden artifacts, iron spearheads, leather slippers, and rings were also found. Local legends say that the *King of Kannauj* with his pregnant wife, their servants, a dance troupe, and others went on a pilgrimage to *Nanda Devi* shrine. The group faced a storm with large hailstones when they disregarded the rules of the land, from which the entire party perished into the *Roopkund Lake* due to the wrath of the local deity.'

The four friends dearly missed a camera here. They peeked into the transparent lake trying to find and locate any skull. Bahadur showed them a few inside the lake as well as took them to a spot where countless bones of homo-sapiens were roughly stacked on each other. Everyone was cautious not to stray near the skeletons and also to keep a safe distance. Pradeep was the first to spot a disfigured leather slipper lying beside them. As soon as Pradeep went on to have a closer look on the slipper, Bahadur behaved superstitious and asked him not to disrespect the dead. He narrated to everyone that the *Hindu* ritual demanded respectful cremation of every demise to free their souls. While the *Anthropological Survey of India* was conducting a study on the skeletons for the last five decades, the locals had always suggested performing spiritual rites and getting rid of the skeletons either by cremation or taking them to the *Anthropological Survey of India Museum* in *Dehradun*. The government of course had been turning deaf ears to their cries except false promises every five years.

THE LAST SURPRISE

Bahadur took out a polythene bag from his backpack. It took a few attempts before him being able to finally open the knot with the heavily gloved hands. There were individual paper rolls wrapping a kind of bread inside. It took a tiny bit of strength to rip off a piece and chewing was tougher. Still, the friends ate their respective roll as Bahadur had promised delicious heavy dinner that night when they get back to his home in *Lohajung*. Byju corrected him by saying *Lohajung* couldn't be reached that night as it was already way past noontime and it took them almost three days to reach the site from *Lohajung*. Bahadur gave a look to Alok and smiled as if denoting, 'it's your time to speak now sir.'

'Yes, we can't reach *Lohajung* today unless we have wings,' Alok winked at Byju.

'What do you mean?' Byju said looking seriously anxious, just like the other two friends standing like a statue.

'That's the ultimate surprise of this journey dear,' Alok said and paused.

The others moved in closer with their eyes wide open. The uncertainty of Alok's personality made the delay part even more unbearable. As the saying goes, "*waiting for the results is actually harder than studying and exams combined.*"

'We'll be hang-gliding our way back,' Alok said convinced that he had taken the smartest decision in the world.

Rohit came forth like a school student in doubt and said, 'what's hang-gliding?'

Alok went to Bahadur, got a booklet, and read, 'hang-gliding is an air sport or recreational activity in which a pilot flies a light, non motorized, foot-launched, heavier-than-air aircraft called a hang-glider. A hang-glider is a type of glider, made from a large piece of cloth fixed to a frame. It is used to fly from high places, with the pilot hanging in a harness underneath using a horizontal bar to control the flight. The peculiar triangular shape makes it easy for the pilot to soar for hours and gain altitude while gliding hundreds of kilometers.'

'Just one question, since when did you lose your mind?' Byju asked.

'Since the time I wanted us all to experience a different kind of adventure,' Alok winked.

'Different here means fatal,' Rohit added.

Pradeep wanted to take over the trek controls now, 'my dear friend Alok! You're not making any sense. Adventure is one thing, but this is suicide. Till now howsoever we enjoyed the trek, but this is too much to ask. I know we vowed our life to friendship, but it was just a metaphor. You are literally asking for our lives.'

'I'm completely being practical here. Mountain ridges are the most perfect point for hang-gliding. Thousands of adventurers have already done this successfully. Moreover, the hang-glider is a safe thing with easy landing and take-off and perfect controls. *Lohajung* is just 18 kilometers away and it will take only two hours' time to reach there by this means of transport. You can ask Bahadur,' Alok spoke in a firm voice and took a deep breath while pointing at Bahadur.

Bahadur was busy untying the glider material from his backpack and sorting out the woven polyester sailcloth. As soon as he heard his cue, he looked at Alok and said, '*sahib ji*, I was saying...' Alok knew what he was about to say and stopped him. Others noticed this and demanded Bahadur's advice. Alok had to give in unwillingly.

'*Sahib ji*, I admit hang-gliding is a popular sport among mountaineers and I myself have done the same thousands of times with tourists, but this is not the place meant for it. In fact, this activity has never been performed past *Rishikesh*, which is more than a hundred kilometers away. The possibility of snowfall restricts this sport here. Also, any altitude higher than this will make breathing extremely difficult and one can even fade while hanging from the harness and let destiny decide the destination. The winds here are always gusty, and all snow-capped mountains look the same. If anything goes wrong, there is no way to get help in midair,' Bahadur said resting his case and going back to streamlining all the aluminum rods as if he knew this won't change Alok's mindset.

'You're saying the same negative things since *Delhi*,' Alok shouted at Bahadur and continued, 'gentleman, we've come here for adventure and the only rule of an adventurous person is to seek more adventure. I've meticulously calculated all the aspects of this sport and it is 100% safe and exhilarating. You three are my best friends and I can frankly tell you that I can sacrifice my life for our friendship. I know our individual lives are different and maybe this is our last trip before we split our focus towards our respective jobs and no longer meet and enjoy together like we did in the last three days. I want to capture each and every moment we can spend in the company of others. I think I'm pretty reasonable here asking for your participation in the final part of our thus-far trekking and going back to our homes with an experience of lifetime that we can tell our grandchildren someday.'

Rohit and Pradeep got emotional and said together, '*bas kar pagle, rulayega kya?*'

Byju playfully screamed, 'NO,' and started running. The rest three ran after him shouting, 'come back you coward.'

Byju was running looking back at his friends with a teasing smile. His friends hand-gestured him to see what's in front of him. He looked forward on time and was able to swerve himself to avoid banging onto the rock that had all the human skeletal bones stacked on it, but he accidentally stepped on the historic slipper. Bahadur saw this, looked up the sky from where he was sitting, pinched his ears, and then folded his hands as if praying to God for forgiveness. He then resumed assembling the hang-gliders. The four friends didn't notice this inadvertent happening to the slipper and continued running after each other playfully. The slipper had turned upside-down.

THE FALL

Bahadur had assembled the hang-gliders. There were four. When asked by the friends, Bahadur told he will fly with Alok and lead the way. Byju suggested everyone flying in a single glider, which Bahadur duly informed not possible due to the small size of the A-frame of the glider where the pilot will be hanging with the help of a harness. Rohit and Pradeep were equally bulky and would not fit together in an A-frame. Even neither one of them would fit with Byju in a single glider. Hence, decision was taken that Bahadur will be with Alok and rest three friends will have their individual glider.

Bahadur instructed them on how to fly and navigate the hang-glider. It seemed very easy, but Bahadur insisted on doing a dress rehearsal before actually taking off.

Alok read from the booklet, 'while in the air, when the pilot shifts left or right, the wings bank left or right and the hang-glider starts to turn accordingly. To speed up, the pilot has to pull himself through the A-frame to shift his weight forward and the glider goes into a nose-down position. To slow down, the pilot needs to push the bar away to shift his weight backward and the glider's nose lifts up slightly.'

It was all in theory and the only practical training they did was hanging on the harness.

'*Sahib ji*, this place is completely different from the popular hang-gliding spots like *Dharamshala* and *Ooty*. Strong winds are always gusting here due to the dynamicity of this peculiar place. Our speed might reach more than we can bear. At that time, we will just have to fly around in circles and try to lower our altitude before moving forward. There might be thermal lift when we transition across *Kalu Vinayak* due to temperature variations in snow and meadows. If a lift is felt, put your weight forward and try to follow me religiously. Keep a safe distance and don't stray too far. Also, if any one of you happens to feel breathless, fading, or losing consciousness, just signal and we will try to land and stop the adventure there,' Bahadur spoke as if he was commanding like a captain. Obviously, he became the real self after finishing talking.

'If you feel nauseated, just throw up as it will turn ice anyways before hitting someone on the ground. Also, it's better to relieve yourself now than peeing midair,' Alok said laughing loudly like *Ravana*. Everyone laughed with him.

Obviously, *Roopkund* was a crater on the mountain face and they needed to reach the sharp ridgeline that towered above. It was *Junargali*. All of them huffed and puffed while pulling their respective hang-gliders up the steep snow-covered incline toward the sky-high end of the ridge. Byju's glider's A-frame got caught on a rock overhang during the final ascent up through snow and Rohit helped reassemble the loosened aluminum rods. There was a small unassuming iron gate peeking over the ridge with its golden bell and flag encouraging them to come say hello. The view was breathtaking with the jagged snowcapped *Mount Trishul, Nanda Ghunti*, and *Chanyakot* staring at them. The ridge itself was extremely thin and pointy allowing only one man to stay at a time. This explained Bahadur's decision to assemble the gliders at *Roopkund* and drag them up here.

Bahadur tied the harness across everyone and thoroughly checked them individually. The four friends were hanging on the harness and holding onto the A-frame. Bahadur asked if everyone was ready. All of them were ecstatic and speechless and Bahadur took it as a yes. He himself put the harness on and hung alongside Alok. Then, Bahadur and Alok pushed themselves backward, stepped on a pointy rock, lifted the frame up, and prepared for take-off. Rohit, Pradeep, and Byju followed him step-by-step and didn't move their eyes off him. A short uninvited wind fluttered the glider fabric. Bahadur seemed unmoved. The wind was strong enough to wave the flag and rang the silhouetted golden bell twice as if signaling them to take the leap now. With two brisk steps forward, Bahadur loudly chanted, '*Har Har Mahadev*,' and they jumped off the left-side cliff drop-off. Pradeep and Rohit followed one-by-one. Byju was still skeptical but decided in a fraction of a second that there was no way back from there and jumped.

The bird's eye view of the whole *Garhwal Himalayas* was simply spectacular. The four friends had never imagined, let alone experience flying like a vulture, and the feeling was utterly indescribable. They couldn't hide their teeth while constantly smiling in a state of bliss. They frequently looked at each other and showed thumbs up. Everyone was exhilarated by taking this way of transport.

Roopkund was behind and Bahadur hand-signaled everyone to look at the *Kalu Vinayak* temple, which they could only judge by the rocks among the white snow carpet. Bahadur and Alok flew around in circles on top of *Pathar Nachuni* before the alpine merged into meadows at *Ghora Lotani* and they continued flying straight. Bahadur was leading the way followed by Rohit and Pradeep at almost equal distance, flying side-by-side, followed by Byju who kept a safe distance from Rohit's glider but also kept on checking Bahadur for signals.

Alok was busy enjoying the whole effortless ride and frequently looking back and singing songs at his otherwise stone-deaf friends. The wind sound and high altitude caused earache to Pradeep who tried to close his ears with his hands, which Alok took as a disrespect toward his singing and stopped looking back.

The flight above *Bedni* and *Auli Bugyal* was long and soothing to eyes because of the dark green color. *Neel Ganga* looked like a long blue snake crawling through the big rocks of *Gharoli Patal*. The boulders looked like pebbles, and the gliders were flying way beyond the height of the centuries' old cypress trees at *Wan* village. They were unable to locate *Ranaka Dhar* nor the exact place where the driver had dropped them because of the lush greenery.

Finally, they were above *Lohajung* and flying around in circles to start the descent at *Ajan Top*. Bahadur maneuvered himself to get the glider in nose-down position. His altitude decreased, and Rohit and Pradeep followed.

Byju, however, couldn't get his glider down. In fact, he had not been able to get an altitude change from the start. He tried swinging back and forth while hanging on the harness in an attempt to point the nose of the glider down. He even tried shaking the A-frame to no avail. All friends had already landed near the *Ajan Temple* and were high-fiving and hugging each other out of happiness and successful completion of the return.

Byju was still airborne and the only thing he could do was revolve around in midair. Bahadur tried waving hands reiterating the landing process to Byju, but the graveness of the situation soon took its toll. Byju noticed something was terribly wrong when the A-frame started trembling as if the aluminum rods were loose at the edges. This could be the reason why the glider was not responding to pushing or pulling the bars. After several failed attempts, it was clear that Byju's hands could never reach the joints at the ends to fix them. Untying the harness was out of the question because the horizontal rod could dislocate and a free fall from this height would definitely be fatal.

Everyone became silent due to the terror scene. Suddenly, a strong gust came out of nowhere and carried away Byju's glider. Byju was helpless in front of this great heavenly power and his face put out an SOS signal. Bahadur started running parallel to the glider while only looking up. After some distance, his foot stumbled upon a rock and he fell. Rohit, Pradeep, and Alok cried in anguish as they all watched their dearest friend helplessly being carried away far across the *Maiktoli Glacier*.

The turbulence had caused Byju's hang-glider to gain altitude tremendously. The speed and distance he had covered by-far was immeasurable. He had stopped trying to disembark and left his fate for the mother nature to decide. Soon, he found himself flying above the clouds with absolutely no visibility below him. The low-to-no oxygen at this altitude made him lose consciousness. His glider was stable and moving steadily when he passed out. The glider ventured endlessly in the vast ocean of clouds towards the sun.

Byju woke up by the infrequent jerks on his ride. It took a while for him to recollect what had happened. He realized that he was still hanging on the glider but this time flying over a dark evergreen forest. The sun was about to set and there was still enough light to see the lush green mountains and valleys everywhere completely covered with virgin forests and no sign of mankind. He was sweating profusely due to him being overdressed for this pleasant climate. He removed his gloves, wiped his forehead with them, and placed them in his pocket.

At the start of the dusk, the glider was slowly descending due to the lack of wind. Byju tried a couple of times to see if the A-frame was working and then just hoped to land on a tree, which would save his life. Suddenly, the aircraft started losing height and the glider was descending toward a cliff. Byju positioned to brace himself when he calculated landing on the short natural runway before the cliff drop-off.

As soon as he stepped foot on the grass, the glider didn't halt and instead dragged him toward the suicide point. He hurriedly tried to untie the harness from his body, but it was too late. The glider got entangled in an overhung dead tree at the edge of the cliff, which was actually a precipice. Byju unfortunately was hanging on the outward end by a small branch. He could see death in the pitch-black darkness that laid far below him.

He was already exhausted by the unforgiving skyride and couldn't take it anymore. He tried his best to pull himself up, but his efforts went in vain when a twig he was holding broke. He fell deep down, and the darkness swallowed him.

The Ugly Alien

Byju woke up from his unconsciousness by the chirping sounds of birds. He slowly opened his eyes. It was dawn. He felt slight headache and shook his head a bit. He was lying on his back and could see the sky-high altitude from where he fell with the hang-glider still caught up in the dead tree branches. He tried to recollect what had happened. It seemed obvious that he had fallen from the precipice but safely landed on a haystack. He thanked God and just laid there for a while trying to absorb the bliss of being alive.

Byju felt something trying to pull his shoe and lifted his neck to see it. It was a mongoose. The mongoose had only one eye with the other one probably damaged by something, and there was a large cutmark over the eyelid. The site of the mongoose trying to bite off his shoe made him scream out loud in panic, which in turn scared the mongoose away.

'Who's there?' A sound came from a nearby hut.

As Byju turned his head toward the hut which was 10 meters away, a girl replaced the bamboo door from inside and came out of the hut. The sun had still not risen completely but the light was sufficient enough to see the alluringly beautiful girl in her late teens coming and standing right next to the haystack close to Byju's feet. It was the most charming girl he had ever seen. Her dress consisted of leaves and grass, which covered her bosom to the knees. She was barefooted and only had a *Rudraksha* mala as jewelry, with nothing on her hands or legs, and unpierced ears. She was a real gorgeous raw beauty. Byju just stared at her and asked himself if it was heaven.

'Who's there?' The girl asked again.

'My name is Byju and I fell from the cliff above. I think I've lost my way. Could you please tell me which place is this?' Byju asked still looking at the girl blinklessly and still lying on the haystack.

'You mean to say you're an alien who has come from another world?' the angel asked.

Byju was surprised. Although, he had been often alienated in schools and colleges of *Delhi* due to his South-Indian looks, "an alien from another world" title was new to him.

'No! I'm just a normal person like you. I'm from *Delhi*. I was riding a glider in the *Himalayas* and a thunderstorm brought me here,' Byju said with an innocent smile due to the silliness of being questioned about him an alien or a normal human being.

'Delhi? Glider? Himalayas? What're you talking about? Have you gone mad? What's your name and who's your father?' The beauty looked even more cute getting pink-skinned and angrily asking questions.

'My name is Byju and my father's name is Venkatapathy Swaminarayan Sivasekharan...,' Byju stopped and then judged that maybe this was a remote village and she didn't know about *Delhi* and all. He continued, 'let's just skip this questioning. Please tell me which place is this.'

'You mean to say you're from another world,' the slim wonder asked.

'Yes! I accidentally fell down the cliff,' Byju tried to shorten the conversation and didn't mind the "another world" terminology as he thought this was the way the girl understood things.

'You got to be joking. What's your name again?' asked the adorable one.

'My name's Byju and I'm not joking. This is serious. I think I'm lost and probably hurt,' Byju replied trying to sit from his supine position.

'Byju? That's a first. Your voice is also different,' the pretty girl paused in confusion to think a bit and then came closer. 'My name is Nayantara.'

Nayantara touched Byju's shoes and then withdrew her hands quickly taking a couple of steps back.

'You said you are not an alien, then how come your feet are different than us,' Nayantara asked cautiously.

At this time, Byju came back to his senses after being mesmerized by the fascinating personality. He looked at her eyes and concluded she was blind as this whole time she had been staring beside him to the rocky mountain and her eyeballs weren't moving at all. Whenever she spoke, she stared at one direction, and would turn her head to listen to him. The blind beauty was still transcendently impressive.

'Ha-ha! These are my shoes. My feet are perfectly normal just like you,' Byju replied chuckling at the comedy of errors.

'What are shoes?' Nayantara asked still maintaining the precautionary distance.

'We put on shoes to cover our feet. Here, I will take it off for you,' Byju smiled at her unawareness.

He wanted to make her comfortable and bent from his sitting position to remove his shoes. He first removed the left leg shoe and sock. He felt slight pain while removing the right leg shoe, but as he tried to pull out the sock, he felt a sharp pain and cried out.

'What is it?' Nayantara asked as if ready to help.

'I think I wounded my ankle on the way down,' Byju said looking at a fresh wound on his right ankle and collaborating it with a thick wooden stick lying on that side of the haystack.

Nayantara came forward and touched Byju's feet. She was both surprised and relieved finding that they were indeed normal human feet. She then proceeded to touch Byju all over. He didn't mind as he thought this was the way blind people greet somebody. Nayantara took some time fiddling with Byju's clothes.

'How come you are so fat, and what's this you're wearing,' Nayantara asked while touching Byju's jacket.

'This is my jacket. I'm not fat. I just happen to wear too many clothes as I was trekking in the mountains,' Byju replied.

Byju took off his jacket as the place was quite warmer than *Roopkund*. He was already sweating profusely as the sun had risen and illuminated the whole area.

'What is a jacket?' Nayantara asked as she continued touching Byju's stomach, chest, hands, and face.

'A jacket is a thing we wear to protect our body from cold, just like we wear shoes for our feet,' Byju replied cautious not to invite another question from this out-of-the-world unaware villager.

'You sound like a grown-up man but don't have a beard and rather have a harsh abrasive skin on the lower part of your face,' Nayantara asked while touching Byju's face.

'That's because I usually shave my beard and moustache, but haven't done so in the past few days,' Byju replied as he tried to drag himself out of the haystack onto the ground.

'What's shave?' Nayantara asked.

Byju couldn't take it anymore. He resorted to not replying and just getting off the haystack. As soon as he touched the ground with his feet, his right ankle gave way and he stumbled. Nayantara got hold of him and lent him a hand to stand up.

'You're hurt. Come, let me take you inside to my father. His name is Netrapal and he is a *Vaidya*,' Nayantara said as she walked Byju toward her hut. Byju seemed astonished that she didn't need any cane to maneuver her way toward the hut, which was 10 meters away and had no clear path but rather some wild grass and small bushes.

Byju entered the hut holding Nayantara's hand for support as he was avoiding putting weight on his right foot. The hut had no windows and was completely made of bamboo including the roof. The architecture was rough and childish, as if someone had just stacked the material together without minding the beauty or the shape. The flooring was of some kind of clay smoothened by hand. The hut was extremely small, maybe 8 x 8 feet, and looked as if the only purpose it served was to provide shelter at night.

A man in his 40s was sitting at the far end of the hut in the corner facing the wall. He was thin and had a beard that looked like it had never been shaved. He was wearing the same dress as Nayantara with leaves and grass covering waist-down. Even after Nayantara and Byju entered the hut, he was still staring the corner wall.

'Father, this man here claims he has come from another world,' Nayantara announced to her father.

'There is no another world. Somebody might be joking with you dear,' Netrapal said to his daughter.

'No father! His name is Byju and his voice and touch are completely unfamiliar to me,' Nayantara justified.

Netrapal stood up and walked to Byju. He started touching Byju the way Nayantara did previously, and Byju soon figured out that Netrapal was blind too. Netrapal asked similar questions about *Delhi*, glider, jacket, and shaving. Byju's reply was also the same as was the case with Nayantara.

Netrapal's fingers thoroughly touched Byju's face as if trying to create a visual image of the appearance. In between the spiked shaved beard of Byju, he figured out the scar-cum-dimple on the cheek.

'You're ugly,' Netrapal said still checking the scar with his fingers.

Byju had gotten mixed comments for his scar-cum-dimple in his life. He remembered in his mind the day when he proposed to a girl in his college and she told him that he was ugly and even a blind man could tell that. Byju thought maybe *Goddess Saraswati* was residing on that girl's tongue that day as her saying came true.

Nayantara giggled as if she already knew this when she initially checked. Byju didn't say anything as he thought there was no use to discuss his looks in front of the blind.

'How did you get this horrible scar on your face?' Nayantara asked.

'I got it when I was a kid. I don't mind it anymore and in fact love it as it resembles a dimple,' Byju replied.

'It's definitely not a dimple. How could you love being ugly?' Netrapal asked.

'Let's just leave it as it is and concentrate on my ankle wound. It is terribly hurting me,' Byju said.

Netrapal inspected the wound by touching Byju ankle and then asked Nayantara to prepare the turmeric application. Nayantara took out turmeric buds from a clay pot kept on one corner of the hut. She crushed the turmeric bud and then started grinding it in between two naturally smoothened stones. She took some water in her palm, which was kept in another clay pot near the stones, to create a paste that Netrapal applied to Byju's wound and covered it with an unknown long leaf that smelled of eucalyptus. Netrapal then proceeded to tie across bundled dry grass to keep the leaf and turmeric paste in place. This was painful but Byju knew turmeric will do good for the wound as it was popular in Indian tradition.

Byju soon judged that Netrapal was a good doctor as he was blind but could still diagnose only by touching the wound. Byju felt relaxed with the combination of the unknown leaf and turmeric powder but still felt a bit pain while trying to move his ankle, to which Netrapal told him that it will take some days to heal as the injury was deep.

Byju asked if he could get something to eat. Netrapal told him that it's not the right time to eat. Byju got confused but then concluded maybe Netrapal meant it was not right to eat at that time with the medicine applied. Byju then asked for some water, to which Nayantara handed him a pot to drink. He peeked into the pot to find muddy water inside and resorted to not consuming anything. Obviously, he thought maybe the blind couldn't see the mud and unintentionally offered him dirty water.

Netrapal asked Nayantara why she hadn't left to collect eatables yet as it was way past the usual time. Nayantara told she was too excited to meet Byju and was looking forward to talking to him and know more about him and the outer world. Netrapal reminded Nayantara that she must do her duties or else the *Pradhan* will get angry. She reluctantly agreed and then proceeded to pick a small basket lying beside the grindstone. The basket was made of roughly bundled dry grass. On her way out, she requested Byju to be there when she comes back because she wanted her friends to get to know him as well.

Nayantara left and Netrapal asked Byju to recline in a corner and relax a bit before he regained the ability to stand and walk. Byju was amused to see how fast Nayantara picked up the basket and left without showing a bit of helplessness of being blind. Netrapal himself started sweeping the floor with his hand and continued till the porch. He was actually inspecting the floor for any irregularities or foreign object, which he threw to the side when found.

Welcome to Taured

After religiously finishing up the household chores of cleaning and rearranging organic utensils, Netrapal sat near Byju and asked him how he was feeling. Byju sat upright and told he was feeling okay and ready to leave. Netrapal was about to give a reply to Byju when Nayantara arrived with her friend.

'Who's this?' Netrapal asked.

'This is me, father. I told all my friends and Mrignayani became too curious to meet Byju, so much so that we came back early,' Nayantara replied.

Nayantara placed her empty basket to its dedicated location and dragged Mrignayani's hand to touch Byju. Mrignayani was an average-looking slim girl with the same dress as Nayantara. The handholding of Nayantara to help Mrignayani reach to touch Byju confirmed that Mrignayani was blind too. Byju first avoided but later gave into this weird welcoming style of the blind.

'Yes Nayantara, you're right. This man is really from the outer world and is ugly too,' Mrignayani said to Nayantara as if affirming to Nayantara's claims.

Byju smirked on being repeatedly called ugly by the blinds. Mrignayani started asking senseless questions one after the another to Byju like what you eat, how come you fly, what's that you're wearing, etc. As soon as Byju opened his mouth to answer Mrignayani, a strong sound of bamboo beating was heard.

'Did you inform anyone else about Byju,' Netrapal asked Nayantara.

'Yes! I informed Sunaina too and she said she will go and inform others,' Nayantara replied.

'That must be Trilochan then asking everyone to gather for *Panchayat*. He must be equally curious,' Netrapal said.

Netrapal stood up and helped Byju stand up. He told Byju that they need to go before the clan where everyone will be happy to meet him and be interested in knowing more about him. Byju was relieved that finally he was going out of the hut and maybe he will find other people who will help him going back home.

Byju clasped onto Netrapal's shoulder in order to walk cautiously and trying not to put weight on his right leg. Nayantara and Mrignayani followed them and were whispering jokes among themselves. The trail had small grasses and very small weeds throughout covered with dried-up leaves and twigs. It was just a 30-meter walk, but Byju found it somewhat difficult walking barefooted as he had left his jacket and shoes in the hut. The other three were quite comfortable and seemed well-versed with the trail as they easily maneuvered their way through the twists and turns, even though they were blind. The last 10 meters had a sharp curve to the left with a large stone placed in one side. The stone had a big *Swastika* carved into it. Byju was surprised to see how everyone turned exactly at the curve and continued the trail.

They finally reached at a clear ground with a huge *Banyan* tree and a stout man in his 50s sitting on a raised stony platform under the tree. A broad-shouldered youth was beating the bamboos fixed on one corner of the raised platform to create the trembling sound. There was a relatively big house made of clay adjacent to the *banyan* tree with roofing and door that of bamboo. There was a huge lotus pond on the left of the big house. Next to the pond, there was a small enclosure with no roof and 4-feet boundary made of bamboo. Straight sky-high mountains covered the whole area and acted as walls behind the pond, big house, *banyan* tree, and literally everywhere Byju could see. Byju turned around to see people coming from other trails toward the clear ground. He could see a hut at the end of one trail, which had different abstractness but similar size and material that of Nayantara's. The centuries' old *banyan* tree was breathtaking and so was the lush greeneries with beautiful thick trees and raw beauty of the place.

Around 40 people gathered the area with almost equal number of men and women. Among them were 6 children between the ages 5 and 15 and only one toddler. Everyone sat on the ground, a few feet away from the stout person sitting under the *banyan* tree. Netrapal, Nayantara, and Mrignayani stood still on the right side of the crowd.

Byju noticed the weirdest sitting arrangement where everybody was facing different directions. All of them were wearing only leaves and grass dresses with a *Rudraksha mala* hanging on their necks and of course barefooted. Byju guessed they were all an unorganized tribe.

There was murmuring from everyone after they had arrived. They were all talking about the rumor just spread about the arrival of a man from outer world. The murmuring became loud and the stout man sitting under the *banyan* tree finally stood up and spoke. He told everyone to be silent and then turned to Netrapal.

'Netrapal, I heard Nayantara has been telling everyone that a man from the outer world has arrived. Is it true?' The man faced Byju while he spoke.

'Yes Trilochan! This man here says his name is Byju and he has come from the outer world called Delhi,' Netrapal replied while holding Byju's hand.

'Byju? That seems to be a made-up name and the whole thing sounds ridiculous! Somebody might be joking. There is no world other than this,' Trilochan said.

'I can say this because I have touched him myself and he is definitely not from here,' Netrapal said.

Trilochan walked close to Netrapal and asked him about Byju. Netrapal held Trilochan's hands and directed them towards Byju. Trilochan started touching Byju on his face. Byju soon realized that Trilochan was himself blind too. Trilochan asked similar questions as Netrapal and Nayantara did and finally made the conclusion that Byju was really a stranger. The crowd just sat still waiting for the result.

'Who are you and what is your purpose here?' Trilochan asked.

'As already mentioned, my name is Byju. I was flying in a glider and ended up here,' Byju replied.

'You can fly?' Trilochan said raising his eyebrow.

'No, it is a glider which we can hang on to and fly with the winds. It got caught in the tree on the overhang there,' Byju said and pointed onto the top of the precipice from where he had fallen. He soon realized his mistake to point out something to someone who was blind, and then just ignored this.

'And what is your purpose here?' Trilochan asked.

'I'm lost, and I want to go back to *Delhi*...' Byju was about to finish his sentence when a loud scream disrupted the conversation.

A slim lady started crying out loud. Trilochan inquired about the reason and she shouted that her toddler was missing. Trilochan got angry asking why she hadn't tied up the toddler's right foot with a bundled dry grass, to which she inconsolably replied that she forgot as everyone started running to the ground after the bamboo beating sound. The toddler was in her hands, but she got so tuned into the questioning with Byju that she didn't notice the toddler slipping away.

Trilochan ordered everyone to find the toddler. Everyone started sweeping the ground with their hand as if searching for something in the dark. Nayantara and Mrignayani along with other girls started calling the name "Kajal," which Byju guessed was the name of the child. They all went into different directions and were walking with babysteps while swaying their hands so as to know what's ahead of them.

Byju was completely blown away from this behavior. He wondered if everyone here was actually blind or just acting. He saw that Kajal had made it to the *banyan* tree and nobody was going that way. He went and picked her up. He then announced the finding. The slim lady came running toward him and fumbled as she took Kajal in her hands and hugged her tightly in motherly love. She thanked Byju. Everyone started clapping except Trilochan who asked everyone to sit down.

'How come you found Kajal whereas we couldn't?' Trilochan asked.

'I looked around and saw her besides the *banyan* tree. That's it, no big deal,' Byju replied with ease.

'Looked around? Saw her? You mean you can see?' Trilochan was frowning.

'Yes of course,' Byju said.

'I don't believe it. You mean you can actually see things,' Trilochan said still unconvinced.

It took a while for Byju to explain his visual acuity to everyone. He started with *Delhi* and for that reason the whole world where everyone had eyesight except a few unfortunate ones. He gave enough examples on what he could see then including but not limited to the mountains, lake, big house, centuries-old *banyan* tree, 40 people in the clan, the children, an old man holding a stick, the trail, the flora, the attire everybody was wearing, *Rudraksha mala*, and so on. At last, everyone was convinced as well as surprised. Netrapal and Nayantara individually asked Byju to reconfirm.

'This is not possible. Nobody in the world can see. This man is lying,' Trilochan shouted.

Netrapal intervened, 'don't be obtuse. You know that our forefathers always taught us that there were people who could see.'

Everyone started murmuring about how they remembered their grandfather or grandmother telling them stories about people with eyesight.

Trilochan verbalized his worries about having around a person capable of seeing and what he could eventually do with these alien powers. Netrapal tried to convince Trilochan that he felt no danger dealing with Byju, to which Nayantara also added that she got no harm while she assisted Byju into her hut. Nayantara's voice was supported by the broad-shouldered young man who was earlier beating the bamboo. Trilochan referred to him as son and finally gave in to the reconsideration requests.

'Byju, welcome to Taured! As you are hurt, I assign Netrapal to take care of you. When the air gets cooler, we will all sit together to know more about your world. Till then, you can take rest. My wife, Drishti, will probably wake up by that time. If she approves, we will let you live here,' Trilochan announced to everyone.

Trilochan went on to ask everyone to continue with their daily chores and routine. He angrily told his son that he will be responsible of the shortcomings if Byju did anything wrong as he wasn't happy with his son contradicting him. As everyone stood up, Trilochan made one last statement.

'And of course, if everything goes well, we will be more than happy to build a hut for Byju and marry him with Nayantara as nobody in the clan is willing to tie the knot with this ugly girl,' Trilochan announced loudly as if wanting to let everyone hear and indirectly tease Netrapal and Nayantara.

Nayantara started crying and Netrapal and Mrignayani tried to console her. Everyone dispersed. Trilochan grasped his son's hand and took him inside the big house. Netrapal asked to go back to the hut. Byju's ankle wound had started bleeding and he thought it would be best to go back to the hut where his jacket and shoes were.

Beauty With A Bump

On the way back, Byju was severely confused about what just happened and was it all real. Where the hell is Taured in a world map? Baseless thoughts came to his mind like he might have died during the glider accident and this was either the afterlife or a dream. Of course, he had many realistic questions that needed answers.

As soon as they got inside the hut, Mrignayani left to collect eatables. Nayantara didn't go as she was still crying but the intensity had lessened after Netrapal comforting her.

Byju had innumerable questions about everything he heard during the meet. He was utterly confused and disoriented about each and every aspect of the place and the people. He wanted answers and Netrapal duly explained.

'Long time ago, my grandfather told me that once upon a time our forefathers had eyesight. They lived in a place called *Nalanda* where they used to study and teach. They had a big happy clan until an invader killed most of them and burnt the whole place. The remaining ran for their dear life. After traveling for months towards the mountains, they finally settled here. Due to something in the environment here, they all began to lose vision and soon became blind.' Netrapal took a deep breath.

'So, you mean everyone here is blind?' Byju asked.

'Yes, every one of us is blind. In fact, we were all born blind and are descendants of blind people for centuries,' Netrapal replied.

'How come you all speak English whereas the language of *Nalanda* was *Sanskrit*?' Byju asked.

'Many, many decades ago, a man had come from the outer world, just like you. His name was Cecil Sullivan and he was different from us in the sense that he never got blind even after staying here for decades. He spoke excellent English and was well-versed in *Sanskrit* too. He taught the natives English and also helped in managing this place by establishing daily routines, walking paths, pottery, and many useful things. He also named the place "Taured." One day, he disappeared,' Netrapal explained.

Byju wondered if the blindness epidemic only affected Indians as Cecil Sullivan sounded like a foreign name.

'So, where did he actually go?' Byju asked.

'You can go and ask...' as Netrapal was replying to Byju, the young broad-shouldered man appeared at the door of the hut.

'Who's there?' asked Netrapal.

'Uncle, I'm Chakshu. I came to meet Nayantara and say sorry about what my father said,' Chakshu replied.

Nayantara was crying softly till then, but her eyes glistened when she heard of Chakshu.

'There's no use son. Your father will never allow you to marry Nayantara because she is ugly,' Netrapal said to Chakshu.

As soon as Byju heard the word "ugly," his memory reminded him of the last statement Trilochan had said. Byju was astonished on how could anyone call such a mesmerizing beauty ugly. As per his judgement, no girl in the whole clan was even close to being as beautiful as Nayantara and one needed to be as blind as a bat to call her ugly.

'Why do everyone call you ugly,' Byju asked Nayantara.

'Because I'm really ugly. Can't you see that?' Nayantara sobbed.

'NO! You are the most beautiful girl in the place. In fact, I have never seen a girl prettier than you in my whole life,' Byju said firmly.

'You are saying this just to calm me. I know I'm ugly because of this horrible scar in my chin,' Nayantara said while lifting Byju's hand and place the fingers to her chin.

Byju first couldn't notice it with bare eyes. Nayantara rubbed his fingers on her chin. There was a mere sensation of some overlying scar tissue. Byju took a closer look and found it was a small healed wound on her chin that was barely visible by naked eyes. He confirmed with Netrapal about it, which Netrapal conveyed as a childhood slip-and-fall injury.

Suddenly, an idea clicked in Byju's mind. He searched his jacket and found the *Mederma* cream that was gifted to him by Rohit. He praised *Lord Shiva* for this coincidence and offered the cream to Nayantara. She was skeptical in accepting the unknown medicine because she was afraid it could make things worse. Byju duly explained about it and Netrapal approved of it. Of course, Byju had to explain how to squeeze to take out the cream and apply it every couple of hours for optimum results. Netrapal understood it as similar to applying turmeric. Nayantara applied it and then ran to Chakshu to hug him. Chakshu hugged her tightly and it seemed like they were die-hard lovers.

'By the blessings of *Lord Krishna*, you will become beautiful again and we will be able to marry,' Chakshu said as he tightened his grip with his strong arms as if never to let Nayantara go.

Everyone became emotional including Netrapal whose eyes filled with tears as he thought of his daughter's happiness. Byju, however, stood there looking at the scene and wondered if God has really created someone special for him also.

Scarcity of Food

Chakshu took Byju to introduce him to the village. It was difficult for Byju to walk, but he someone managed with the strong handholding of Chakshu as well as his excitement toward this mysterious place. The name of the village, "Taured," didn't find a place in Byju's geographical memory. It was something he hadn't even heard of before. He asked Chakshu, but Chakshu was clueless too about the outer world and why this place was named like that.

Byju asked Chakshu to explain more about Cecil Sullivan, to which Chakshu told Byju that he didn't know much other than he drowned in the pond one day. One thing he knew was everyone had strict daily routines to follow and needed to do their specified work.

Chakshu explained, 'the various stages of the routine are determined by my bamboo beating. When the chirping of birds starts, it means everyone should get up and start collecting fruits and leaves to be brought to the preserving jar, which is kept near the *banyan* tree. It is the one that is also used for the beating for different announcements. When it feels the hottest, I would beat the bamboos, and everyone deposits the collectables in the preserving jar. Then, we all need to take bath near the pond. After that, everyone gets their share of food and can relax till the air turns cooler. I would beat the bamboos again and everyone gathers at the *panchayat* ground to hear religious songs or stories from my mother, Drishti. At last, we all go to relieve ourselves and then return in our respective huts to sleep. Of course, there are some exemptions to certain individuals in this routine like my family because we are the keepers of the village as well as others like children, elderly, Netrapal because he is a *Vaidya* and needs to be available always, and Sunaina because she is the designated potter.'

Byju understood that the concept of day and night didn't exist here as it is always dark for the blind, and they just calculated the appropriate time according to the temperature in the air and chirping of the birds.

Byju told Chakshu that he was hungry, to which Chakshu replied that it was not the time. Everyone ate only once during a sleep-wake cycle and Byju will come to know about that. Byju was famished but his curiosity about knowing further about the place soon took over the hunger.

While they were both walking and discussing things, the lady who had lost the toddler earlier came out of her hut toward the pond and filled in some water in her clay pot. Byju asked Chakshu and Chakshu explained this was the only source of edible water. This explained the dirty water in Nayantara's house.

Chakshu felt it was time and started beating the bamboos of the preserving jar. The noise was loud enough to call everyone who came from everywhere with some carrying fruits and only a single kind of leaves with them. They duly put all in the preserving jar, which already had some stock from before. The crowd then went near the pond to take bath.

Netrapal asked Byju not to bath as it will affect the wound, to which Byju agreed and went to sit at the raised platform under the *banyan* tree. All females moved into the enclosure with around 4-foot boundary wall made of bamboo. The enclosure was open toward the pond where they picked up water in their clay pot to bath. Men bathed in the open. Nobody dared enter the lotus pond and always kept a safe distance while picking up water. Some had even brought new set of leaves and grass to change their dress after bathing.

Chakshu was quick in bathing and came back soon to Byju as he was too excited in meeting the outsider. Byju asked Chakshu what was the purpose of the enclosure for females when nobody could see in the village. Chakshu reiterated to Byju that the only method of moving around and knowing a person is by touching, and the enclosure served the purpose of restricting uninvited males to stray and touch females while they were bathing. Byju smirked as he felt idiotic in asking this stupid question.

Everyone sat at the *panchayat* ground near the *banyan* tree like they did when they first heard of Byju. Trilochan started announcing names and individuals came near the bambooed preserving jar where Chakshu took out a single leaf and placed two different fruits on it for them to carry and eat. The procedure continued till all 40 got the same. Kajal, the toddler, was also counted as a person while distributing, which explained her mother getting twice as she was breastfeeding. Sunaina was also provided an extra set to take to her hut for her ailing grandmother who couldn't come to the ground to eat. At last, Chakshu handed the leaf and fruits to Byju as well.

Everyone ate slowly, thoroughly chewing the food and enjoying the flavor. Byju watched them curiously as they hit the bigger fruit softly onto the ground to break it open and then consume what's inside. The smaller fruit was eaten directly and had a couple of big seeds inside. Lastly, they ate the leaf and then went inside their respective trails, probably toward their huts, to relax.

Though Byju was extremely hungry, he wanted to ask Chakshu about what the fruits and leaves were before consuming them. Chakshu told him that the bigger fruit was called "*bael*," which had a hard surface cover just like eggshell. He needed to hit it softly on the ground to break it open and then savor all the contents. Byju did as Chakshu told and ate the content, which was a combination of jelly and sweet.

Next, Chakshu told Byju that the smaller fruit was called *"chikoo."* It had a hard surface initially when collected but softened as it was stored in the preserving jar for a few days, after which it could be eaten directly. It contained two or three big seeds inside, which were inedible. Byju ate *chikoo* and felt the extreme sweet taste. Finally, Chakshu told him that the leaf was called *"paan,"* which needed to be taken as a whole by chewing slowly and then swallowing. Byju felt a peppery taste while chewing the leaf and then gulped it.

Byju acknowledged Chakshu that the names and flavors of the delicacies were the same as it was in the outer world, though the colors were different and that was why he couldn't recognize them before.

Byju asked Chakshu from where they get the fruits and leaves. Chakshu replied the sky God threw food for them. Byju looked around and saw some fruit-bearing trees and creepers overhanging the mountain walls. He figured out the blind obviously couldn't see the trees and only collected what's fallen on the ground.

Byju asked for more as he was still far from satisfied after eating the small meal. Chakshu warned Byju that it was a sin to ask for more food. Byju tried to persuade Chakshu, to which Chakshu reminded him that he had already told him about food being provided only once in a sleep-wake cycle. Byju tried to reason with Chakshu about him not being familiar with the village rules and sufficient food provided three times a day in the outer world. Chakshu was unmoved and further reasoned about food being scarce in the place during different seasons and the policy was made for sustenance of all. Byju felt no use in trying to convince the committed keeper of the place.

Netrapal asked Byju to come and relax in the hut till the air got cooler. Chakshu advised the same as Byju had obvious difficulty in walking during the whole time. Chakshu stayed at the *panchayat* ground attending to the children who wanted him to play “rock balancing” with them.

Netrapal and Nayantara took Byju to their hut. Netrapal reapplied turmeric and medicinal leaf onto Byju’s ankle wound. Nayantara too applied *Mederma* cream on her chin as Byju had instructed her previously. Byju was feeling lightheaded by the brainstorming so far and fell asleep for an afternoon nap.

The Prediction

Byju woke up by the feel of soft hands trying to push him slightly. He could also hear the bamboo beating sound. He opened his eyes and saw Nayantara trying to wake him up.

'Wake up! Drishti aunty has arrived and wants to meet you. Come, let's go,' Nayantara said.

Byju stood up and held the hand of Nayantara who assisted him in walking and pacing to the *panchayat* ground. It was the start of dusk. As they reached there, a slender woman was sitting under the *banyan* tree wearing the same dress as other females, just a bit dried though. She had her eyelids closed. The eyelids looked like they were hollow from inside. Trilochan and Chakshu were standing next to her. Everybody was coming and touching her feet as a sign of respect before sitting in front of her. Byju figured out that there was a pattern in sitting arrangement as everyone sat on the exact location every time they are all there. Maybe they developed an understanding not to crash on each other and designate a place for daily rituals. Nayantara also went forward and touched Drishti's feet before coming back to her location.

Chakshu asked Byju to come and seek the blessing of his mother. Byju initially relented but later gave into the beliefs of the locals. As Byju came close to Drishti, she stood up and started touching Byju. Byju was familiar with this stimulus as was the case with every other person he encountered in the village. Drishti, however, didn't ask any question and sat back in her place. Byju stood there and waited for Drishti's response who started whispering a *mantra* in *Sanskrit* to herself. After some time of fiddling with her *Rudraksha mala*, she stood up and addressed the gathering.

'I sense corruption. I sense theft. I sense mutiny. I sense fire destroying our heritage. I sense deceit. And, I sense death,' Drishti said in a firm voice.

Everyone stood up and started murmuring about the prediction. Trilochan asked everyone to sit and calm down as he will handle the situation.

'From the moment I touched Byju, I knew something terrible is going to happen. Now, Drishti has also confirmed the same. I ask for everyone's opinion in what should be done now,' Trilochan said.

Byju intervened by arguing that it was just a prediction that could prove wrong and that he only came there by accident and meant no harm to anyone. Every single person raised his/her voice in conveying the clear message to Byju that Drishti's prediction had never gone wrong and what she said will definitely happen without any doubt. Even Netrapal and Nayantara looked worried as if already suspecting Byju.

Chakshu recommended giving more time for him to be with Byju and understand his thoughts. Chakshu's words meant the same value for the villagers as his mother's. Of course, Trilochan and Drishti couldn't neglect the trivial wish of their son. At last, everyone settled for not letting Byju sleep inside anybody's hut for they thought he brought some kind of curse with him. Drishti didn't speak anything else during the whole time.

They all started chanting the religious song, "*darshan do ghanshyam naath mori ankhiyan pyaasi re*." Chakshu was beating the bamboo even harder to create a thumping effect while the voices collectively grew louder and louder.

Afterward, Trilochan announced that he and Sunaina, the potter, had devised a technique by which they can preserve the touch and feel of an individual even after his/her death. Sunaina brought forth a skull made entirely of clay. Of course, it resembled the face of Trilochan, and Byju easily judged that Trilochan was taking joint credit for a thing probably made by Sunaina alone.

Trilochan took the skull to everyone who frisked and confirmed that the touch and shape felt like that of Trilochan's. Trilochan grinned, which was one of the rare expressions in that mysterious village. Trilochan got so happy that he announced his son's marriage with Sunaina. Everyone got ecstatic except the few well-wishers of Nayantara. Sunaina herself was surprised and helplessly sad for her friend. Nayantara wept soundlessly.

Trilochan didn't want to miss this opportunity of rubbing salt on Netrapal's wounds of giving up hope for his daughter. Trilochan further announced that Nayantara will be married to Nilayan, another young man from the community who had way too many scars on his face and had one white cornea. This made Nayantara's weeping develop sound. He finished by saying the pre-marriage ritual will take place the next sleep-wake cycle.

It was turning dark and Byju found it difficult to see anything. He saw everyone going back into the pitch-black darkness that laid upfront. Trilochan and Drishti also went into one of the trails toward the village holding a small clay pot each with water inside. Byju didn't know what to say to Chakshu who looked terribly sad and heartbroken. He was following his parents into the trail. Byju guessed it was the time for them to relieve themselves before getting into their hut to sleep.

As Byju watched everyone disappear in the woods, he felt the horrible sensation of being alone in the darkness. He could only figure out the *banyan* tree in front of him and climbed it till he reached on top of a branch that was thick enough for him to spend the night there. He looked everywhere and could see nothing but absolute darkness, even above him, and wondered how the natural places that look so beautiful in the daytime get so horrific during the night.

Byju was famished, tired, and scared. After some time, he even heard the sound of someone coming back from the trail toward the big house. He wondered if it was Trilochan, Drishti, and Chakshu coming back. He couldn't sleep thinking about his odds of surviving the night. The fact of *banyan* tree being haunted and considered to be home of ghosts in the Indian tradition kept him awake the whole night. He soon remembered that it was the only kind of tree in the whole world that gave out oxygen at nighttime too, so his chances of death due to suffocation was ruled out. Ultimately, he slept on the thick branch of the centuries' old *banyan* tree.

The Telephone Invention

Byju woke up horrified by a nightmare. He had a dream of the villagers trying to kill him by strangling with dried grass. He rubbed his eyes and saw that it was the start of dawn. The visibility was enough to see nearby surroundings. It took a while for him to recollect the series of events till now and realize that he was sleeping on a wide branch of the huge *banyan* tree. He yawned and stretched as he lifted himself to get to a sitting position. He felt a pulling sensation on his clothes and turned his head around to find the one-eyed mongoose nipping on his t-shirt. He got frightened and shooed the mongoose. He climbed down the tree and went near the pool. He just stared at the lotus pond thinking should he drink from it or not. He was parched, took a handful of water, and drank. He threw up the water instantly. The sound created by this commotion woke up Chakshu who slid the bamboo door of his hut from inside and came out.

Chakshu asked Byju what happened, to which Byju told him about his inability to drink the pond's water. Byju asked if he could get clean water by any means, to which Chakshu firmly replied that the pond's water was the one and only source of purest and holiest water in the village. Byju weighed the dangers of getting dehydrated or drinking dirty water and judged it would be best for him to avoid drinking it.

Byju asked Chakshu about the one-eyed mongoose. Chakshu replied that when he was a kid, there were many instances of stumbling upon a snake, rat, or other small species of animals. Then came the season of famine and drought when the sky God only dropped dry leaves or branches and even the pond dried up completely. The villagers somehow survived the hardship, but countless dead animals were identified throughout. After it rained for a season, life resumed as usual and no further animals were ever felt alive. Maybe, the mongoose was last of the species.

Byju told Chakshu that he wanted to “answer the call of nature.” Chakshu advised Byju that he should have control over his body’s functions and postpone the defecation process until after the sermon before going to sleep. Chakshu explained the dilemma of his morning routine in the outer world as opposed to the strict rules of this strange place.

Chakshu went inside his hut and brought a clay pot for Byju, which Byju filled with water. They then walked the trail toward Nayantara’s hut. The hut’s door was closed as it was still the early phase of dawn. They continued following the trail. It was a zig-zag trail and a bit darker than outside mostly because of the dense overhanging bamboo trees. There was a sharp curve to the right and a large stone was placed there with a huge “*Shankh*” carved on it. The stone was atop a somewhat raised platform, which was twice as large as the diameter of the stone. They further followed the trail 10 meters and stopped in front of an elongated clear area of land approximately 15 x 50 feet. The land was muddy and kind of dug up everywhere.

Chakshu confirmed if anyone was already there by asking out loud. There was nobody of course. Chakshu then told Byju to go and relieve himself, to which Byju was confused as to where and how. Chakshu explained one needed to find a place which had not recently been dug up. Then, he/she needed to dig up a hole to the length of the elbow and finish the excretion by filling up the hole with soil after them. Byju inquired about the possibility of digging up somebody else’s feces during this process. Chakshu laughed off by saying one needed to wash hands after coming out of the *Shauchalay*.

Byju was disgusted by the whole protocol and requested Chakshu to go back to the village as his desire to empty his bowels had been tarnished by the potential scenario. Chakshu reconfirmed and then suggested following the trail further as it would ultimately lead to the *panchayat* ground itself.

They continued for another 30 meters or so and then there was again a sharp curve to the right with another huge stone placed there, but this time the stone had an *"Om"* carved on it. Immediately after the curve was another hut made of clay with bamboo roof and door. It was of similar size that of other huts in the village except that it was artistically created with equally smooth edges on each side and a beautiful porch complementing the view. The hut's bamboo door was closed as the birds hadn't started chirping yet. There was a pile of clay accumulated near the hut and some unfinished clay pots lying nearby. Chakshu confirmed that it was the house of Sunaina who was the designated potter of the village. Byju added that he knew she was the one who was going to marry Chakshu, to which Chakshu got frustrated and told Byju that he loved only Nayantara and will only marry her.

Chakshu and Byju continued on the trail till they reached to another sharp right curve with yet another huge stone placed there, which now had a *"Trishul"* carved on it. Going further, they came out the dense greenery toward the bathing enclosure followed by the pond, Chakshu's big house, and finally at the *panchayat* ground.

They sat under the *banyan* tree. Byju could see that Chakshu was disturbed upon Byju's commenting on Sunaina being Chakshu's bride-to-be. To change Chakshu's mood, Byju asked him about how they fell for each other and what were the ups and downs in their love life till now. Chakshu's eyes glistened as he spoke about Nayantara.

While finishing up his long speech on the various romantic encounters with Nayantara, Trilochan came out of the hut and stretched his arms and legs. While Chakshu and Byju were busy discussing the rare love story of a remotest village, they didn't notice that the birds had started chirping and the dawn had converted into full-fledged morning.

Chakshu and Byju secretively moved toward the pond as Trilochan came to the *banyan* tree. Trilochan paid his obeisance toward the tree for assigning him as the keeper of the clan and also toward the preserving jar for safekeeping the fruity treasures.

Chakshu whispered in Byju's ears that he wanted to share something with him that he had never disclosed to anyone as he didn't think anyone was worthy of telling this. Byju was all ears. Chakshu told him that he had invented a system by which he can talk to Nayantara anytime and nobody would ever know. Byju asked Chakshu how it was possible.

Chakshu took Byju inside his hut. It was the biggest one in the village with two separate rooms. Chakshu held the hand of Byju while quietly inching toward the second room at the end of the corridor. They both got inside with Byju only catching a glimpse of Drishti sitting erect in the middle of the first room facing the wall.

As Chakshu invited Byju to enter his room, Byju inquired about Drishti sitting in the other room, to which Chakshu replied that his mother was always in deep meditation and woke up only for a few hours per day.

Chakshu brought Byju into a large room with a lot of stuff scattered everywhere. It was a complete mess and Chakshu told Byju to sit on a raised surface denoting his bed till he picked up the thing that he wanted to show him. It was both a bit shadowy and unfamiliar place for Byju, so he decided to stand in a corner near the door.

Byju took out two small bowl-shaped clay pots with a single small hole at the bottom of each. Chakshu inserted a silky thread through the hole into the small clay bowl and then tied a knot to secure its location inside. He then took the other end of the silky thread and did the same with the other small clay bowl. One could easily judge that it resembled the cup phones in the normal world, ditto!

Chakshu handed one bowl to Byju, walked a few steps back to straighten out the string, and asked Byju to place the small clay bowl over his ear. Byju already knew what was going to happen but didn't want to kill the spirit of this overexcited scientist. Chakshu spoke softly some words on the small clay bowl that he had placed over his mouth and Byju responded by announcing what the words were. Chakshu behaved like he was high on ecstasy. Byju congratulated him on this great invention and asked how he thought about it. Chakshu told Byju that he had named this invention as *Durbhash*.

There's No Way Out

Chakshu explained in detail how day and night he only thought of conversing with Nayantara and listening to her sweet voice. One day, he found children balancing the small bowls. Chakshu accidentally picked two bowls kept on each other with their bottoms attached and raised them to his ears. One child requested Chakshu to give it back, the voice of whom came right across the bowls. This gave the base idea for the invention, which took many years to develop until one day Chakshu found a group of worms with a kind of hairy body. The hairs from them when held together created a string, which created a vibrating sound. Chakshu then swept the whole village with his hands to find similar worms. Finally, he found enough to create a small length, and that was the first time he used it. Chakshu told Byju convincingly that he will keep his search on till he was able to create an appropriate length that would reach up to Nayantara's hut from his room.

Byju got impressed by Chakshu's persistence and hard work and promised to play a major role in getting the lovebirds together once he went out of the village and brought back his friends. Chakshu revealed to Byju that there was no way out of the village. Byju first related to Chakshu that everyone here was blind and there might be a simple climb up somewhere. He was now feeling better and would be able to climb even with the limp. Chakshu told Byju that no one had ever gotten out of the village. In fact, he himself had been to each and every corner of the village and thoroughly checked everything. There was absolutely no way out.

Byju was taken aback by the firmness in voice of Chakshu. His thoughts of getting his ankle ready and go back to his home were completely blown apart. He couldn't accept this and started running around. Chakshu didn't stop Byju as he also knew it was the bitter truth. Byju followed the trails everywhere and checked all the straight mountains. He even climbed a few trees and check on creepers that were not going up to the top. He realized that it wasn't a valley but a basin. The mountains acted as walls standing erect and massively tall. He inspected each and every aspect of the village and got terribly frustrated and sad. He climbed on a tall tree and sat on a branch watching everyone do their respective job of searching for fruits lying on the ground with hand-sweeping.

Even when Chakshu beat the bamboos to call everyone for lunch, Byju didn't show up. After everyone went to their respective huts to relax, Byju returned to Chakshu at the ground and sobbed like a baby. Chakshu recommended him to accept the inevitable. Chakshu even offered Byju that he himself would ask Sunaina to build a beautiful hut for him. Maybe, Byju's rare power of seeing could help him find silkworms and finish his dream of connecting with Nayantara via *Durbhash*. This made the moment even sadder for Byju, who felt extremely helpless and just asked for some time alone. Byju climbed onto the *banyan* tree and reached his previous location where he slept the last night. He laid there and wondered how the tables had turned against him.

Chakshu was upset too. He never had a friend as his father never allowed him to. Trilochan had always told Chakshu that he will one day become the *Pradhan* of the village and he should never befriend anybody or that might lead to losing his position. Chakshu saw a friend in Byju and wanted his help in dealing with the situation of getting married to Sunaina instead of the "apple of his eyes," Nayantara.

Chakshu also understood that this was as a bad phase for him as it was for Byju as Byju himself was trapped in an undesirable place for life.

Some children came to Chakshu to play with him. Chakshu told that he was not feeling like playing. The children insisted and Chakshu instructed them to play "Hide & Seek." One child stood with Chakshu while others ran in different directions. After a few seconds, Chakshu let the child go and seek others. Byju watched this from the *banyan* tree and smiled broadly with sadness and tears in his eyes.

Chakshu just sat on the raised platform with hands on his head. Byju laid on the thick branch of the *banyan* tree and stared up above him the sky through the branches and leaves. He soon felt asleep due to the stress.

Byju woke up due to the shouting of Trilochan on Chakshu. Trilochan was asking Chakshu to beat the bamboos to call everyone for the evening program. Chakshu wasn't obeying. This commotion made Drishti to step out of the hut and convince Chakshu that it was for his good. Though unconvinced, Chakshu went ahead and beat the bamboos as per his mother's wish. Everyone soon came to the *panchayat* ground and sat in their typical location with atypical facing directions.

Trilochan ordered Sunaina to come forward. Trilochan asked Chakshu to come near Sunaina. Upon sensing no response, Drishti went to Chakshu and pulled him softly near Sunaina. Drishti made sure that Chakshu touched Sunaina's face. Chakshu said, 'I feel nothing.' Drishti took it as a yes and announced Chakshu's approval. Then, Drishti asked Sunaina to touch Chakshu's face. Though Sunaina also seemed uninterested as she was a friend of Nayantara, she knew that she couldn't do anything apart from doing what was asked of her. She didn't touch Chakshu's face but whispered to Drishti that it was okay. Drishti announced Sunaina's approval as well. A couple of random elders were called to the front to check both the girl and the boy, who touched and appreciated the beauty of both of them and declared everything felt perfect. Then, Trilochan and Drishti touched Sunaina's face and approved of her also. Drishti further announced that Sunaina's grandmother was bedridden and couldn't attend the evening sermons anymore, so she assumed it will be a yes from her as well. Hearing both the parties' approval, everyone clapped and praised *Lord Krishna* for the blessing. Trilochan announced the marriage will take place the next sleep-wake cycle. A tear rolled down Chakshu's eyes.

Next, Trilochan asked Nayantara to come forward. Nayantara and Netrapal were already standing on one corner as they always did. Nayantara was hugely depressed and her face down all the time. With a heavy heart, Netrapal dragged his daughter near the raised platform. Trilochan then asked Nilayan to step forward, which he happily did. They were then asked to proceed with the touch on face and approval protocol. As Nilayan tried to come near Nayantara, Nayantara just ran away toward her hut. Netrapal wanted to follow her, but Trilochan ordered him to stay.

Trilochan expressed his anger in Netrapal's daughter not participating in the sacred activities of the villagers. This followed a long speech by Trilochan on how the population of the village had been continuously declining over the past decades due to the extremely low fertility rate among women and marrying according to elder's wishes was the only way to maintain sanctity of the village. This made everyone angry and loud murmuring of disagreement and dismay aroused toward Netrapal. Hearing this, Trilochan silenced everyone and asked Nilayan if he was interested in marrying Nayantara anyway. Nilayan agreed.

Trilochan lectured, ‘everyone knows Nayantara is ugly and so is Nilayan. Marriages are made in heaven and they both are made for each other in respect to their ugliness. Nayantara can’t expect herself to run away from this and stalk Chakshu who is respectfully going to marry Sunaina as per his parents’ choice.’

Trilochan finally announced that he had no other option but to order Netrapal to forcefully get his daughter married with Nilayan or the whole village will. Everyone clapped and praised Trilochan. Netrapal went back to console his daughter. Mrignayani followed Netrapal. Chakshu stood there like a statue, maybe sensing his dark future ahead.

Drishti started reciting *Shlokas* from the *Mahabharata* and explained the parts on how *Dhritarashtra* was born blind because his mother, *Ambika*, got frightened due to the scary appearance of *Ved Vyas* and closed her eyes during the union. Also, when *Gandhari* was forced to marry *Dhritarashtra*, she resolved to spending the remainder of her life blindfolded in order to share the debility of her husband. Afterward, *Gandhari* got so frustrated due to her unusually long pregnancy period that she pounded her stomach and a grey mass came out. *Maharishi Ved Vyas* divided the mass into 101 parts and stored in earthen pots to incubate. First to be born among these was *Duryodhana*, followed by 99 brothers, and one sister, *Dushala*. *Dhritarashtra* also got frustrated of *Gandhari’s* delay in birth of his sons and had another son, *Yuyutsu*, from his maid, *Sughada*. *Yuyutsu* was the only son of *Dhritarashtra* who survived the *Kurukshetra* war.

Byju watched as everyone disappeared in the dark trails. Byju’s mind was too occupied with his own destiny that he just prayed to *Lord Shiva* to help him get out as well as help the poor souls marry their loved ones.

Byju was feeling restless but couldn't do much in the dark. He felt hungry and looked below him toward the preserving jar. Though it was dark, shapes were visible due to the moonlight. Byju noticed Trilochan and family get back to their house after relieving themselves.

Byju climbed down and sat inside the preserving jar. He started eating but couldn't stop with a couple of fruits as he had not consumed sufficiently in the past two days. He was not feeling sleepy and knew that if he got his belly stuffed, he might feel lazy and ultimately sleep. This worked and Byju slept in the preserving jar.

The Grave Well

Byju woke up due to the pain of a sharp bite on his elbow. He opened his eyes and found the one-eyed mongoose next to him in a standing position. He saw bitemark on his left elbow. He angrily threw a *bael* on the one-eyed mongoose, which the mongoose dodged and ran away into the dark trail toward Nayantara's hut.

It was the early dawn with not much visibility and birds hadn't started chirping yet. As Byju lifted himself to stand up, he felt the urge to go and relieve himself. He got out of the preserving jar and stared at the trail that would ultimately lead him to the *Shauchalay*. It was completely dark due to the dense overhanging trees. He also thought about the possibility of digging out somebody else's feces and this time he even won't have the water pot with him. He concluded on sitting by the pond to answer nature's call. He finished his business there and used pond's water to wash himself.

Byju then started his searching for the way out. He tried climbing an erect mountain to no avail. He then proceeded to inspect each and every mountain wall to check for possibilities. His search didn't yield him any result, but he decided to die trying rather than losing hope. Time passed on till it became hot in the afternoon and he heard the bamboo beating.

Byju went to the *panchayat* ground for lunch but found everyone standing in a circle around Trilochan and expressing their concern about discovering human waste by the pond, which had led to contamination of the holy water. Trilochan was sure that this was done by Byju, but Chakshu argued that there was no proof. Trilochan asked Chakshu to get Byju, to which Chakshu told him he didn't know where Byju was.

Trilochan asked everyone to get the food, to which everyone disagreed as they had not taken a bath and it was against their culture to consume food without bathing. Trilochan was able to convince them by saying that he will consult Drishti on this, but that can only be done when the air got cooler. They finally settled with providing food to the mother of the newborn and Sunaina's grandmother. As soon as Trilochan bent down to pick up deliverables, he fumbled on the skins and peels of the fruits.

He shouted in distress that some food had been stolen from the holy preserving jar. The crowd startled and then became restless. Trilochan loudly announced that without a doubt, this was all Byju's doing. He expressed him being concerned from the moment Byju entered the village and now it was beyond any doubt that this intruder had come to destroy their civilization. Chakshu intervened by again saying there was no proof and they should rather calm down and ask Byju before taking any decision. Trilochan ensued the conversation by declaring that there was no need for an investigation or proof here as their system had been running perfectly for generations and this isolated event was the brainchild of an alien. Chakshu further argued that Byju claimed to have seen a mongoose around and that mongoose could have done it. Trilochan ignored this and preferred interrogating Byju first. Everybody agreed and Trilochan ordered them to go and catch Byju. As everybody went in different directions with some sweeping the ground with their hands, some walking in babysteps, and some trying to climb trees. Trilochan came close to Chakshu and whispered in his ears that he didn't want his son to be declared a traitor of the community, so it was for his better to stop taking Byju's side.

Upon hearing the orders of Trilochan to catch him, Byju had already left the spot because he knew Trilochan was against him from the first day itself. Byju had climbed the *banyan* tree and sat on the thick branch thinking nobody would guess or spot him. Trilochan just sat angrily on the raised surface and Chakshu stood beside him. Rest were all over the village except Netrapal, Nayantara, and Mrignayani who were still unconvinced about Trilochan's allegations.

It got dark and everyone was standing in the *panchayat* ground waiting for Drishti to come out. As Drishti came out of the hut with eyes closed perpetually, everyone first touched her feet to show her respect. Drishti took her seat and then went into chanting "*Om*" for a while. She then took a deep breath and told everyone that Byju was up on the *banyan* tree. Byju was taken aback from this revelation. His expression resembled, 'this is cheating.'

Everyone gathered around the *banyan* tree and the strongman Nilayan, who was both visibly and tactually ugly, climbed up the tree toward Byju. Byju could easily guess that there was no way he would be able to fight off Nilayan. Also, there was no way further up, and below was a mob waiting to catch him probably to deliver a capital punishment.

Byju calculated his odds of jumping onto Chakshu's hut and surviving the fall. As Nilayan reached his hands to get a hold on Byju, Byju jumped over the big hut. Amazingly, he landed on the roof which was made of bamboo and was too dense and strong to bear his weight easily. Unfortunately for Byju, Nilayan landed on the roof when he also jumped in an attempt to catch Byju. Nilayan barely missed a large piece of rock kept on the roof probably to keep the bamboo in place. After a few attempts of running in circles on the roof, Byju had reached a dead-end where he could see the angry mob had already surrounded the Trilochan's hut completely not leaving any scope to escape.

Nilayan lifted the heavy rock with his strong arms and threw it toward Byju. Byju easily dodged and the rock hit the mountain wall on the back of the hut. The collision caused a spark, by which fire caught onto the bamboos. The fire soon engulfed the whole roof and some dry grass kept inside the hut as well. Nilayan had already jumped off and saved himself. In the raging fire, Byju had no other option left but to surrender himself. He too jumped, and the villagers caught him.

The villagers had probably never encountered a fire in their life and did nothing about it other than keeping a safe distance from the heat and moving on with the proceedings. Chakshu advised on getting water from the pond and pouring onto the hut, which was let down by Drishti stating nobody should touch the contaminated water. While the raging fire engulfed the whole hut, the villagers concentrated on Byju's prosecution.

Drishti was straightforward in asking Byju for his stand and explanation on the allegations of contaminating the holy water, stealing food from the preserving jar, and now burning the central hut. Byju feared for his life and lied that he didn't know anything about the contamination. As for the theft, he had already told Chakshu of a one-eyed mongoose straying around, which could have done that. The hut catching fire was not his fault as Nilayan threw the rock, which caused the spark.

Drishti angrily stood up and shouted that Byju was a liar. Drishti told Byju loudly that the contamination was caused by him alone, the fire was a result of him running around in the first place, and even the blind knew mongoose don't eat fruits. Byju was speechless. Drishti sat down and requested Trilochan to announce the punishment.

Trilochan sentenced that though he would have liked to avoid the bad *karma* of sentencing a punishment but rather would have liked to exile Byju from the village, as there was no way out from the village, he had no other option but to declare the harshest punishment on him, one that had never been sentenced before – to be thrown into the "*Shamshan Kua*." Some cheered in joy of getting rid of this uninvited guest, some were shocked about the sentencing, some were neutrally silent, and the well-wishers of Byju were pensively sad.

Byju was confused and asked grinning Trilochan about what exactly was *Shamshan Kua*, to which he replied, 'you will come to know once you get there.' Chakshu begged his father to reconsider the penalty as that was a place where all the dead people are disposed of. Byju overheard this and panicked.

Nilayan held Byju tightly and a few other remorseless individuals lifted Byju and took him into the dark trail toward Nayantara's hut. Everyone else followed. Though it was already dusk, and the trail should have been otherwise dark, the sky-high flames of the burning hut made everything quite visible to Byju and the long shadows of so-called prosecutors of the place made the entire scene horrific.

They all continued the trail in front of Nayantara's hut and stopped at the large stone with "*Shankh*" carved in it. Nilayan single-handedly slid the huge standing stone with his massive strength. As the stone was moved from its position, Byju noticed that there was a pitch-dark hole that was about 2 feet in diameter. It seemed like the raised surface was created to mark it and the stone was intentionally placed on top to suffice as a cover. Without a second thought, the men lifting Byju threw him into the hole. Byju screamed as he was swallowed by the darkness, but then complete silent prevailed both inside and outside.

The Yellow Sapphire

Byju slowly opened his eyes, blinking constantly. He first saw a blur image of something staring at him close to his face. He soon realized that it was the one-eyed mongoose again, but this time just an inch away from his face. He screamed in fear and lifted himself up. The mongoose squeaked and then ran away. Byju was too dazed and took some time to recollect the events and stand up. He looked above and around 15 feet above him was the hole from which he was thrown. There was reflective daylight coming through the hole, which provided some visibility inside.

Byju looked around and could see that he was in an underground cave, which had a large area but mostly rocks and mud. Climbing up to where he had been thrown from was out of question as it was too high and there was nothing to help him get there. He even blindly ventured in a couple of natural small tunnels, which only led to dead-ends and made him return back to the main large cave. Eventually, he just sat in the middle, exactly where he had fallen, and stared up and around.

Byju remembered Chakshu saying to Trilochan that this pit was used to dispose of the dead. He jumped from where he was sitting and looked at the ground. He used his feet to disperse the mud and dust present there and found some pieces of small bones indicating that indeed the dead people were thrown in here. It seemed nobody had been thrown in recently.

Byju roamed around and searched everywhere. He couldn't find any way out and all the short and long tunnels had dead-ends. He was afraid of going into the small tunnels on his knees as he was afraid of stumbling upon a snake or any other creature. He concluded that he was going to die in the cave.

Byju came to the middle and started kicking and dispersing the ground in anger. He realized that there were hard things under the mud that didn't look like bones. He picked one up and it was a big necklace that was old and had an antique design. He thought of throwing it away but then placed it in the pocket, for he saw the unique design that signified luck. For a moment, he thought of further exploring the spot for valuables, but then logically thought the uselessness of wasting energy as he was going to die inside the cave for sure.

Byju just sat on the ground holding his head with his hands in depression. He heard the giggling sound of the mongoose and saw it sniffing and staring at Byju from a distance. Byju guessed the mongoose used to eat the dead people thrown in the cave and was waiting to gorge on him after he was dead.

While sitting, Byju looked around in frustration and couldn't find a rock to hit the mongoose. Instead, he saw the small pile of mud created by his exploration earlier and lifted a handful to scare the mongoose away. As soon as grasped the mud pile firmly, he felt something inside it. He opened his fist and searched the content. He saw a long rectangular piece of "*pukhraj*," the size of two fingers of a grown-up man. He gently cleaned it and it was shining like a diamond, just a bit yellowish though. Light coming from the hole gleamed inside the cave because of the buffed *pukhraj*. Byju was amazed with this marvelous piece of gemstone but looking around soon realized that he was still trapped, and these might be the last pleasures God gave him before taking his soul.

Byju laid there with the yellow sapphire on his chest and himself looking up the hole opening way up. He had stopped trying to search for a way out and resorted to just lie down and die of starvation. He could hear and feel the presence of mongoose wandering nearby, but kept saying, *"abhi hum zinda hai."*

Suddenly, Byju had an afterthought. He remembered everyone throwing him inside the pit. Then, he fell down and became unconscious. He asked himself, 'why would they throw the mongoose after me?' He remembered Trilochan's statement that nobody had ever notified about the presence of a mongoose in the place, but he had seen the mongoose. Wait a second! The mongoose was only encountered when it was early dawn and the birds hadn't started chirping. That meant, the mongoose roamed in the place only at nighttime most probably to eat the nocturnal insects. In the daytime, the mongoose just went into its burrow. The mongoose was here in the cave, so the burrow must be ending in the cave.

The logic was clear. A burrow has two parts. If one part was ending inside the cave, one must be opening onto the village. The burrows are usually not straight but slanting downwards. So, to go up to the village, he needed to incline upwards.

Byju stood up and adjusted the yellow sapphire to reflect the light towards the mongoose. The mongoose ran into a small tunnel and Byju followed on his knees. The tunnel was earlier avoided by Byju, but this time, he felt confident following the mongoose as it would have definitely eaten any snake in the route.

Byju saw an opening on the roof of the tunnel end, through which the mongoose disappeared. Byju used his hands and the yellow sapphire to dig up. It was relatively easy as the soil was damped and Byju just had to scratch the roof to get most of the soil fall onto the ground. Byju followed the slanted trail upward as he constantly removed the soil around the burrow with the gemstone to make it large enough for him to get through. At last, he saw light at the far end.

Byju's hand came out of the burrow. He softly removed the mud around the hole and finally pulled himself out. He dusted off the mud from his hair, face, and hands. His t-shirt was wet and completed soiled. He saw the haystack and looked up in the sky to realize that this was the place where he had initially fallen from the cliff. He was skeptical about going into Nayantara's hut but decided for it as he trusted this family and also needed to get his jacket and shoes from there.

Byju quietly ventured near Nayantara's hut and peeked inside. He noticed Chakshu and Nayantara sitting inside with Nayantara's head leaned on Chakshu's shoulder, and Nayantara's tears rolling all over her face. It seemed as if both hadn't slept last night and cried the whole time. Nayantara was blaming herself to have informed everyone about Byju's presence in the first place. Chakshu was trying to calm her by saying that there was nothing they could have done to save Byju. Byju felt comfortable revealing his rebirth to these good Samaritans and entered the hut.

Chakshu and Nayantara were extremely happy in finding Byju alive. Chakshu asked and Byju explained how he came out of the "grave well." Byju saw Nayantara's kind affection toward him and took the necklace out of his pocket. He gave it to Nayantara to wear and revealed that he found it inside the cave. Chakshu explained that there are stories of their ancestors wearing malas other than *Rudraksha*, and this must be from someone who was wearing it when she died, and they threw her into the pit with it.

Nayantara wore it and was looking like a queen. Byju hoped Chakshu could see this, but Chakshu instead touched Nayantara to check on the necklace. He commented it as rough and bumpy, which of course it was, as necklaces are generally worn for visual delight and not tactile.

As Chakshu was frisking his hands on the necklace and told Nayantara that it added to her ugliness, Chakshu touched on Nayantara's scar and then rubbed the surface softly. He was blissed in informing Nayantara that he couldn't feel the uneven surface as before and that she was surprisingly beautiful again. Nayantara checked on the scar herself and appreciated the same.

As she jumped in excitement, Byju saw that the scar was not there and asked Nayantara if she was using the *Mederma* cream religiously this whole time. Nayantara confirmed as her father was a *Vaidya,* she knew the importance of following the treatment regime. Byju congratulated them on the great achievement. Nayantara and Chakshu hugged each other tightly and thanked God for sending Byju and removing this curse.

Byju asked Chakshu to help him get out of the village. Chakshu told Byju that the previous night his mother whispered in his ears to go and remove the stone lid of the hole where Byju had been thrown. Drishti also told Chakshu that she sensed happiness for her son and the oldest woman in the village changing Byju's destiny. As the happiness portion had been achieved, Byju asked Chakshu to explain the second half of his mother's statement. Chakshu guessed that it must be Sunaina's grandmother, Sonakshi, who used to recite stories about Cecil Sullivan during sermons when Chakshu was a kid, and that she must be knowing something that nobody else knew. Also, as an added advantage, everyone was at the *panchayat* ground helping to rebuild the big hut and only Sonakshi was at home as she was too old to move around. Byju put on his jacket and shoes and asked them to not waste time then.

Scene 20

THE PRESERVING JAR

Chakshu, Nayantara, and Byju went into Sunaina's hut where Sunaina's grandmother, Sonakshi, was lying atop a haystack, which denoted a bed. Next to her was a clay wall with a lot of small vertical lines drawn on it that were all equal in length with horizontal lines crossing a few. Sunaina was not there as she had gone to help in constructing the big hut. Nayantara introduced Byju to her and she was equally excited and told Nayantara that Sunaina told her about Byju and she was curious too to meet him. Chakshu explained the situation.

Sonakshi tried to lift her up to a sitting position. Byju helped her and Sonakshi spoke.

Sonakshi told that her father was the *Pradhan* of the village when Cecil Sullivan had arrived. The big hut belonged to them at that time and Cecil lived with them for many years. The whole clan was unorganized and wild, blind of course as they were since after the *Nalanda* era. Cecil helped them establish routine in the way of collecting food, utilizing water, settings rules, wearables, toilet, etc. He even introduced their family with pottery that helped tremendously in collecting water and building huts. He placed stones at the four corners of the village to mark the trails. Time spent with him helped everyone get accustomed to his language and that soon became the primary language of the place.

Chakshu spoke in between and added that if Cecil Sullivan was alive today, they all might have been way more developed than they are presently. Byju inquired on how Cecil died, to which Sonakshi replied that it was not the truth. In reality, he got out of the village and her father recommended keeping this as secret and relaying the message of Cecil's death in the pond so that nobody in the village would develop a false hope of escaping the village themselves.

Chakshu agreed that his grandparents also told him that Cecil Sullivan's body was never found, and he drowned in the pond.

Byju asked Sonakshi on how Cecil Sullivan got out of the village as he wanted to get out too. Sonakshi told Byju that she was going to reveal the secret to Byju only because Byju could see as Cecil did and the deadly way up could otherwise prove fatal to the blind.

Sonakshi explained that the place had a tendency for famine and drought every 25 years. When she was young, the pond dried up completely during one such season. The pond was rather deep, about two human size standing one on top of the other. It was created by their ancestors who first came to settle there centuries ago. The dried-up pond led everyone to enter it to get water available in small patches here and there.

One day, Cecil came to Sonakshi's father and told him about a crevice between the mountains at the far end of the pond, which was not otherwise visible from the shoreline. Two straight mountains joined there and had a crevice formed, which was not visible from the distance or the angle but could easily help a person climb up to the top. Sonakshi and her father went with him to inspect the crevice. Cecil asked her father to tell everyone and he will assist in them climbing. Her father disagreed due to the dangers involved and asked Cecil to go if he wished to. The next day, Cecil disappeared, and her father spread the rumor of a deep whirlpool at the far end of the pond which sucked Cecil and he drowned. This ensured everyone staying away from the pond. After the season ended, rain filled the pond again and till now no one had ever gotten into the water.

Byju asked Chakshu to go toward the pond and try the unknown route. Chakshu expressed his concern that the pond was filled with water and that it was indeed deep. Byju sadly agreed and expressed his dismay over not knowing swimming. Chakshu asked what swimming was. Byju told him about it, to which he was amused on how a man was able to swim and fly in the outer world. Byju told him that there was not enough time to explain everything and he expected Chakshu to get him out of this life-and-death situation.

Chakshu asked Sonakshi when the pond will dry up. Sonakshi thought for a moment and then tried to stand. Chakshu and Byju helped her. Sonakshi touched the wall where there were innumerable small vertical lines with horizontal lines striking some of them. She inspected thoroughly and then calculated with her fingers. She announced that the famine and drought season was not due for another 12 years. Chakshu was amazed on her talent of counting days and calculating years and season. Byju, however, couldn't agree to wait for 12 long years before he could climb his way out.

Chakshu and Byju asked Sonakshi if there was any other way Byju could get out. Sonakshi seemed reluctant, but upon the requesting of Nayantara too, she spoke. She disclosed that Byju might have noticed that the preserving jar had a peculiar shape. The shape was that of a thing that could float on water, and the two beating bamboo sticks help in navigating. Byju rolled his eyes and visualized the preserving jar. Yes, it looked like a circular boat and he had also been inside it.

Sonakshi said before Cecil went ahead to climb, he pursued her father to come along with him. When her father declined the offer, Cecil instead made the preserving jar and told her father that this will help to reach to the crevice in case her father ever changed his stand. Of course, her father didn't tell the villagers about it and it had never been used that way.

Everyone thanked her and came out of the hut. They made a plan and whispered something in Nayantara's ears. Byju hugged Nayantara and wished her all the happiness in her life. Nayantara thanked Byju for everything and conveyed that she truly believed Byju was sent there to help her from her miseries.

THE GREAT ESCAPE

Nayantara ran toward the *panchayat* ground and went to Netrapal who was standing at his usual location. She intentionally whispered loudly in Netrapal's ears that Byju had come out of the "*Shamshan Kua*" and was sitting near the *Shauchalay*. Somebody from the crowd overhead this and shouted aloud to inform the others. Everyone ran toward the trail to *Shauchalay*. While running on the trail, Nayantara held Netrapal's hands and took him to their hut.

Trilochan sensed something was not right and stopped halfway in the trail to think.

Byju and Chakshu were hiding behind the female bathing enclosure. They quietly stepped toward the *panchayat* ground and ultimately came to the preserving jar. Drishti was sitting under the *banyan* tree meditating. Byju conveyed this to Chakshu whisperingly, to which Chakshu replied that she didn't get disturbed by anything and only spoke when she felt the need.

The decades-old preserving jar took some time and effort to first empty it off the eatables and then dislodging it from the ground. It was heavy due to the thick bamboos used for its construct. Byju and Chakshu grasped opposite ends and tried to lift and carry to the pond.

Suddenly, a hand clutched Byju's shoulder. Byju turned around and saw it was Nilayan. Byju told Nilayan that he just wanted to go from the village and nothing else. Nilayan was emotionless and pinned Byju down. Byju could see Trilochan standing near Drishti under the *banyan* tree. Byju tried his best but couldn't get Nilayan off him.

Chakshu grabbed Nilayan from behind and threw him a few feet away. Nilayan literally was in the air for a few milliseconds when Chakshu lifted him off Byju and threw him. Nilayan stood up and dusted him off. Nilayan's white cornea and scarred face made him look like a demon. He was damn ready for a fight with Chakshu as he always saw a competitor in him. Chakshu cracked his knuckles and got ready too as he knew the only reason Nilayan was willing to marry the otherwise ugly Nayantara was to defeat him.

Nilayan and Chakshu both ran toward each other and started fighting vigorously. Both were equally strong and young, and their battle seemed never-ending. At one point, Chakshu pinned Nilayan down and shouted at Byju to drag the preserving jar toward the pond. Nilayan soon took over and the fighting ensued.

Byju dragged the preserving jar to the shoreline. He saw Nilayan overpowering Chakshu. He thought for a second and his heart became reluctant in trying to escape while poor Chakshu was fighting with the devil. Chakshu was hurt badly and bleeding from his face. Nilayan's relentless attacks had gotten Chakshu completely exhausted. Chakshu was clearly losing and taking the severe beatings all on himself.

Byju saw the villagers coming from the trails. He had to make the choice real soon. It was his last chance of escaping from the village before villagers would catch him again and throw inside the deadly pit. He may not survive it this time. Byju closed his eyes for a moment and then made the choice. Moreover, he never had a fight with anyone as his friends used to call him names for him being too weak and avoidant.

Byju ran toward Nilayan with bloodshot eyes. He kicked Nilayan strongly and Nilayan flew some distance before hitting the big hut. Tears rolled down Byju's eyes as he helped the battered and bloodied Chakshu stand up. Nilayan hand-swept his nearby area and found a large piece of stone that he used both of his hands to lift. As he lifted the stone up above his head and was preparing to throw it on Byju and Chakshu, Trilochan felt Drishti's hand trying to hold his hand. Trilochan shouted, 'STOP.' Nilayan paused but still had the large stone on him lifted and ready to be thrown.

All the villagers who had already reached there became silent.

Drishti stood up and announced that she sensed Byju had brought back a piece of jewelry that once belonged to the queen of the village centuries ago. He had given it to a beautiful girl who will be the future headwoman of the place. This gesture of Byju shouldn't go unrewarded; and therefore, he should be allowed to leave as it was for the best.

Byju and Chakshu got delighted upon hearing this judgement. Nilayan kept the stone down and stood there shocked. Trilochan was unimpressed and wanted to go toward Byju, but Drishti held his hand and said whisperingly, 'no.' All the villagers got surprised of the revelation and came to Drishti to touch her feet. Drishti further asked them to come with her to meet Nayantara. She left while pulling Trilochan's hand to go with her and the rest villagers followed. Only Chakshu and Byju stood at the *panchayat* ground.

Byju hugged Chakshu for everything he underwent because of him. Chakshu told Byju that he appreciated the blessing Byju brought in his life by getting him close to Nayantara again. As Byju and Chakshu walked toward the preserving jar kept at the shoreline of the pond, Byju joked to Chakshu that he could see there are some scars on Chakshu's face because of Nilayan's beating and it would be on Nayantara to decide if she wanted to marry an ugly Chakshu. Perhaps, Trilochan could make an exception for his own son and force Nayantara to marry Chakshu. They both laughed as they pushed the preserving jar into the pond.

Byju gave an interlocked-thumb handshake to Chakshu while standing inside the preserving jar. Byju took out his t-shirt and gave it to Chakshu. He told him that the threads from it will help Chakshu complete his invention of the *Durbhash*. Chakshu told him that it was no longer required, but Byju insisted on giving it by stating that his help in inventing the wonderful thing could be considered as a gift from him to the villagers. Chakshu smiled and accepted it.

Byju bid farewell to Chakshu. Byju then picked up the bamboo sticks inside the preserving jar and started navigating toward the corner at the far end of the pond. Chakshu folded his hands and said, 'thank you for your visit. I'll be your *darshanabhilashi* forever!' Both Byju and Chakshu grinned with tears rolling from his eyes. Chakshu stood there as Byju paddled the makeshift boat to finally arrive at the corner where indeed a crevice was present, approximately 2 feet in width, that zigzagged its way up to the top of the cliff. Byju looked at Chakshu one more time who was now sitting and splashing water from the pond to his face to clean the aftermath of the fierce battle. Byju just waved his hands and whispered to himself, 'goodbye my friend.' He started the climb.

It was late afternoon when he started. He climbed and climbed. There were a few moments when he felt exhausted and just stopped to take deep breaths with his feet firmly held over the zigzag turns of the crevice. The sun had already set, and it was the start of dusk when he finally arrived at the top of the cliff. He was exhausted and just laid there to catch a breath. Then, he stood up and saw the pitch-dark underground, which was invisible from the cliff. He thanked *Lord Shiva* and then looked on the opposite side of the cliff to find the glider still hanging from the dead tree at the precipice. He walked all the way semi-circling the basin to reach the precipice.

Initially, he was afraid to go to the end to detangle the glider, but then looked around and saw darkness starting to engulf the area and little time left for him. Soft breeze of wind started. He carefully detangled the glider and then reassembled all the parts firmly ensuring no loose rods this time. Luckily, the sailcloth hadn't been torn from anywhere and it was still airworthy.

He looked around and saw a small hill at some distance that glistened under the moon. He lifted the glider on his shoulder and climbed the 45-degree ascent of 100 meters. It was an easy climb as compared to the other climbs he had previously undertaken onto the erect mountains.

He reached the summit and noticed that it was perhaps the isolated highest point surrounded by forests. It was the perfect spot for the hang-glider to takeoff. He checked the rods once again and found the vertical one loose at the joints. He looked up the sky and spoke, '*ab kya bache ki jaan loge*.' He then tightened it again and then proceeded to takeoff without a second thought. As he jumped from the cliff, he shouted, '*Har Har Mahadev*.' Soon, his glider started flying and disappeared in the darkness ahead.

The Lottery

Byju woke up to find himself hanging on the harness and his glider flying above the clouds. The sun had partially risen. He pulled and pushed himself to no avail. This time, he wasn't going to let go easily, so he dislodged the already loose vertical rod and then started hitting the rod going to the nose-tip of the glider. After repeated attempts, the rod accidentally tore the sailcloth and the glider nosedived into the clouds.

After crossing the clouds, it went straight down toward a deep canyon with a river flowing in it. Byju noticed that he was going straight into the gorge. There was no respite and he was going straight down in the river. He panicked but was helpless with his glider achieving breathtaking speed. He shouted, *'bhains ki aankh'* and then closed his eyes as he dived into the river.

Byju's eyes opened for a moment when he saw the blur image of a person talking over the phone and explaining that he had seen the number on the wrist and describing the person he found. Byju couldn't figure out much words except *"Sherpa"* and *"Kali Gandaki River."* Byju was too dazed and went into sleep again.

Byju opened his eyes slowly. He was inside a hospital room. He had plaster on his right leg and bandage on his forehead. He had an ECG monitor applied on his chest and intravenous saline water infusion via an overhanging bottle. He found it difficult to move and just laid there looking at the roof. He soon heard voices of people coming toward him.

'What do you mean unsaleable,' Pradeep spoke as he stopped right at the entry door of the hospital. Some murmur was heard through his phone of somebody speaking from the other side.

'I don't care. I've myself confirmed this from my links at the Gemological Institute. It is a rarest of the rare precious stone and should be at least 100 times what you are offering.' Pradeep was shouting despite being shushed by a hospital staff.

Again, some murmur heard through the phone.

'Don't worry about the police, my father will take care of that. Just look for a worthy and wealthy buyer,' Pradeep said as he hung up.

Pradeep came inside the room and saw Byju's eyes opened. He ran outside and called Alok and Rohit.

All three friends welcomed Byju back and told him how happy they were to see him alive. They told him that he was missing for a few days and they searched everywhere and thought of the worse, but by the grace of *Lord Shiva*, Bahadur called and told them that he had been found. There was nothing to worry. Byju had broken a few bones while his dive into the *Kali Gandaki River* and may need to spend a few days in the hospital.

The next few days went with Byju taking rest at his home and all his three friends coming daily and spending quality time with him. Byju told them everything he had gone through and they were amazed.

Byju inquired about what Pradeep was talking over the phone, to which Pradeep informed him that he was talking to Choksi, an underworld gem dealer, and making a deal with him to sell off the *Pukhraj* as soon as possible as the *Nepal* police found the yellow sapphire in Byju's pocket and were making inquiries about the discovery. Even *Delhi* police had inquired about the same as they got some kind of insider information about a precious stone being found. Choksi had informed Pradeep that it was a huge more than half-a-kg and 4-inch long piece of *Pukhraj* that had never ever been found or even told of in the past. The carat itself was more than 3000. It was impossible to get a buyer as this one hell of an item would get the whole law enforcement departments chasing them. So, the final offer was XX crores and he suggested they finalize immediately to avoid any trouble.

Byju initially didn't want to let go of the thing that helped him escape, but then gave in at the insistence of Rohit who had already dreamt of the things Byju could buy with XX crores. Alok also suggested to stay out of the trouble in carrying an expensive gemstone for long. Byju finally agreed. Pradeep quickly redialed and instructed to deliver half the amount in cash and the rest half as donations from at least three foreign countries towards his father's NGO that looked over the widows of *Varanasi*.

THE SPECTACLES

After a year, vanity vans were parked outside *Hotel The Royal Plaza*and a press conference had been arranged. The board outside displayed, "Book Signing by Bestselling Author – Byju."

Byju and Rohit arrived in a brilliant black *Audi A8*. The 5-star property had enough staff to properly manage the journalists' rush inside their "*Venetian*" hall with a lot of round tables and one small but highlighted dais. Everyone stood up and clapped as Byju entered the hall and walked up to the dais. They all took their seats with Byju standing on the dais and folding his hands to say, 'namaste.'

A young reporter asked, 'sir, we heard rumors about your accident while on a trek. Please comment.'

Byju smiled softly and replied, 'Accident? No, it was the destiny. The spread of the alleged rumor helped in my book's sales and it became the bestseller. Sometimes, God plays games to open our eyes.'

A slim girl asked, 'why did you change the book and what happened to the previous book on social issue?'

'I no longer want to write on social issues. Instead, I made a tiny change in the title by adding the word "Literally," and have resorted to writing story-based novels instead,' Byju said.

There was a general silence in the room. Byju sensed there were no further questions. As Byju went on to sit on a chair at the dais for book signing, a voice diverted his attention.

A middle-aged expressionless reporter spoke, 'One last question sir. The story in your book closely resembles your life with exact match of the turn of events like your trekking, disappearance, and you becoming rich. Is this novel fiction or non-fiction?'

Byju noticed it was the same reporter who was active in his press conference held last year.

Byju took some time to think in his heart and make the judgment. All eyes were on him. He was judging on the consequences of nobody believing his tall claims versus him lying harmlessly. Finally, he announced, 'fiction, fiction of course.'

The middle-aged expressionless reporter said to his colleague while leaving the hall, 'I knew it. It is too strange to be true.'

Byju was all smiles as he started greeting and signing individual books of his fans standing in a long queue.

Rohit helped everyone with the directions on the way out and where to dine.

After everyone went from the hall, Rohit came to Byju and congratulated him. Byju looked onto the wall in front of him. Rohit noticed a poster and started reading the quotation from it as this time it was clear to him. Byju stopped Rohit by placing his hand over his mouth. Byju took out spectacles from his shirt pocket and wore it. The poster was now clear to him and he read the quotation aloud - "the only thing more terrifying than blindness is being the only one who can see." — José Saramago."

Not Again

Byju was driving the caras well as talking to his mother in *Malayalam* over the speakers connected to his phone via *Bluetooth*.As Byju finished the call, Rohit asked Byju the possible reason why everyone was blind in Taured.

'I told you I can't be sure as I'm no doctor or scientist.But, one thing I noticed and recollected from my memories there is that there was no direct sunlight inside the village.The place was a basin and the sun's rays never touched the ground because of the huge mountains covering from all the sides, though there was enough visibility due to the reflection.The fruits and leaves were all faded in colors and may be lacking in vitamin A, the essential nutrient for our eyes.The prolonged deficiency may have caused the generations to go blind by birth itself.'Byju replied.

'Then, why not Cecil?'Rohit argued.

'Well, maybe the epidemic only affected the Indian race.There are many examples in our day-to-day life where we see people being immune to some deficiencies.For example, a person who is always slim even though he eats a lot and doesn't exercise at all, whereas a person who eats very little and does a lot of exercise gains weight,' Byju tried to reason with Rohit.

'*Bhai*, that sapphire made us rich.You said you gifted the necklace to Nayantara.Do you think there are chances we might find more of the treasure inside the well?'Rohit asked smiling broadly.

'Yes, there could be.In fact, I sometimes think of people who devote their life to finding even the minutest piece of a valuable item, and then there are these places where treasures get lost forever,' Byju replied.

'*Bhai*, what I meant to say is...,' Rohit was about to complete when the car stopped.

'I know you more than you know yourself brother.I know what you want to say but let me clarify this loud and clear to you, there is no worldly reason that can ever get me even close to a deadly adventure again,' Byju spoke as he waved hi to the Nepali gatekeeper.

Rohit saw that they were in front of Alok's house.Byju reminded Rohit that it was Alok's birthday and this time Rohit forgot about it.They noticed Chaudhary was sitting with his *hookah* near the park and wearing *lohi* shawl.The Nepali gatekeeper opened the main gate for the car to be parked inside.Byju got a huge giftwrapped box from the boot of his car and walked straight inside the main door.Rohit followed.

They all stood encircling a small but expensive round glass table with a small chocolate cake in the middle.Rohit lit the sparkling candle placed on top of the cake, which had Alok written in white color and a happy birthday plastic tag.Byju, Rohit, and Pradeep sang, *"baar baar din yeh aaye, baar baar dil yeh gaaye, tum jiyo hazaaron saal, yeh meri hai aarazu."*

The three friends sat in the much-coveted living room.They heard the tappingof the champagne glass with a spoon and Alok came in front.

Alok said, 'time for my birthday speech.As you all know that for me, you're the only three friends I have from my childhood.In the last four years since we all passed out from *Venky College*, we only meet occasionally and that makes me feel damn lonely.I know that we all have different family obligations and our lives might not necessarily be together...'

Byju stood up and interrupted the speech, 'wait-wait-wait!I know where this is going.Sweetheart, this time I'm 200% sure I don't want to go on a literal breathtaking adventure again and for that reason not on any trip.'

'But this one's different,' Alok raised his voice.

'WHAT?' Rohit and Pradeep said as they stood up in shock.

Byju came close to Alok and said, 'I know I pledged my life to our friendship, *partune to dil pe hi le liya yaar*.'

Alok was unimpressed.He saw Rohit an easy target and asked him to select any one finger by showing three fingers of his right hand.Rohit selected the middle one.

'Ah!I knew it,' Alok said happily.

All the three friends stood still with stoic expression.Finally, Pradeep politely asked Alok to explain.

Alok softly replied, 'the ring finger was for spending a night in *Nidhivan*. The index finger was for an underwater expedition in *Bhimkund*.And, the middle finger is a simple trip to...'

Alok paused a bit before revealing the secret.The rest three held their breath and closed in for the final surprise.

Alok finally announced.

'THE SENTINEL ISLAND.'

Pradeep opened the gate wide open and ran toward the park climbing the railing and jumping off.Chaudhary watched him and stood up with his *hookah*falling down.The Nepali gatekeeper first saw Pradeep run and disappear in the woods and then heard a squeaking sound of the car coming out of the house.Byju was driving the car and sped away toward the open end of the *Tilak Nagar*street.After a couple of seconds, Rohit came out of the main gate and ran after the car shouting, '*BACHAO*!'

The Nepali gatekeeper and Chaudhary watched this scene in amusement and scratched their heads.They then looked toward the balcony of the house where Alok was standing and laughing out loud.

THE END

Bonus Scene

Bahadur takes out a piece of a newspaper article from his jacket with his gloved hands.It has Byju's photo in the main page along with the luxurious car.He tears it vertically and throws the pieces into the limitless depth of the cliff from the drop-off where he is standing.

Byju is standing at the iron gate of *Junargali*.The flag is fluttering vigorously because of the strong gusty wind that is making a loud whoosh sound.He rings the golden bell and looks back at the *Roopkund Lake*.He then buckles up the harness of his hang-glider and gets in position.Finally, he jumpsinto the darkness shouting, '*Har Har Mahdev.*'

www.ingramcontent.com/pod-product-compliance
Ingram Content Group UK Ltd.
Pitfield, Milton Keynes, MK11 3LW, UK
UKHW040009200726
13854UKWH00001B/118